T.M. FRAZIER

Cover design by T.M. Frazier
Cover model Travis DesLaurier
Edits by Love N Books

A Quick Note About Reading Order

This book is the seventh and FINAL book in the King series. You must read the six prior books in order to fully appreciate Preppy, Part Three. King, Tyrant, Lawless, Soulless, Preppy One, Preppy Two, and Preppy Three.

Acknowledgements

I honestly don't know where to start. Thank you so much to my husband for being a true source of inspiration to me every single day. Thank you for pushing me to always do my best and supporting all the times when I can't do my best in other areas. I wouldn't be writing if it weren't for you. I wouldn't be happy if it weren't for you. You are an amazing person and I'm so lucky you chose me.

To Sunny, Kim, Clarissa, Pam, Louise, Kara, for taking the time to read early copies of this book. To Jessica for putting up with my weirdness and for reading my scribbles out of order and for encouraging me every step of the way. Thank you to Julie for keeping me sane and for just always being there. Thank you to my agent, Kimberly Brower, for sticking with me through this series.

A super special thank you to Rochelle Paige. Someday I hope to be as good of a friend as you are. And THANK YOU to Beth Ehemann for being my writing buddy during this process. YOU ARE MY HERO!

Thank you to Ellie for making my words pretty and for putting up with my ever changing deadlines.

Thank you to my daughter for smiling and laughing and being a light in my life when some days seem creatively dark. YOU are why I do this. I want you to grow up and chase your dreams like Mommy chased hers. I love you, sweet girl.

Thank you to Frazierland, my readers group. YOU guys keep me motivated. Every day you remind me of how much I love what I do. Thanks for hanging out with me. Laughing with me. And being ridiculous with me. I look forward to all of our good times ahead.

Dedication

For my readers

"The boundaries which divide Life from Death are at best shadowy and vague. Who shall say where the one ends, and where the other begins?"
—Edgar Allen Poe

PROLOGUE

DRE

THERE'S THE TYPE of evil that dwells deep within men's souls, the kind that makes them do cruel things because they're driven to do so by the demons whispering inside them.

Evil can be subjective.

At least that's what I've learned in my time with Preppy.

Not all acts of malice are created equal. Not all men who have those demons choose to unleash them into the world. There are those like Preppy, like Bear, like King, who've chosen to channel that need, compartmentalize it into something they only draw upon when needed.

When threatened.

Preppy is capable of both cruelty and mercy, of both murder and salvation. He's been the victim, the villain, and the hero. What I don't think he'll ever realize is that this gives him a power most men would dare not aspire to. Throughout his entire life, he's walked a fine line between heaven and hell, between sinner and saint, between endless love and hardened hatred.

Then he died.

And although his death didn't include ceasing to breathe, he still found himself in a living hell.

Preppy had every reason to harbor resentment so deep there would be no coming back from that dark place. He could have let the devil turn him into one of those men who answers his demons without question.

I don't want to say Preppy had been tamed. Tame is the last word I'd use to describe him. He's too wild. Too unpredictable.

Too Preppy.

Taming Preppy would be like trying to put a leash on the wind.

However, he did have this eerie sense of calm about him. He became focused. Precise. If you looked past the smile and jokes, you'd see someone who held his cards close to his chest and knew when to play them.

Like now.

With the echoes of my son's cry playing over and over again in my head I knew Preppy would come for me. He'd play those cards.

And he'd win.

They say the road to hell is paved with good intentions.

The way back will be paved with blood.

CHAPTER ONE

DRE

I WAS JOLTED into consciousness, my head slammed against the side of whatever confines I was trapped in. I opened my eyes, but nothing but blackness stared back at me. The occasional bump and hum of an engine made me realize I was in some sort of vehicle, but I wasn't in the cab.

I was in the trunk.

My hands and feet were bound together. A gag was tied so tightly around my head the fabric prevented my mouth from closing, so I was forced to bite down on it.

My heart was beating a million miles a minute. I felt my fingers turned cold. I felt dizzy, and when I tried to swallow, I found that I couldn't.

Don't panic.

I took a deep breath and set a mental image of Preppy and Bo in my mind. An acute sense of focus took over. A determination to get out of that trunk and back to my family.

But how? Eventually, someone was going to open the trunk, I had to be ready.

I felt around with my fingertips and bare feet for anything I could use as a weapon but disappointment set in quickly.

It was empty.

Out of frustration and fear I pounded my bound wrists against the coffin on wheels, pausing when I remembered something.

"Andrea, how did the cat end up in the trunk of the car?" my dad asked.

"I dunno," I sang innocently, twisting from side to side as my dad hit a button on his key chain, popping the latch. Mr. Wiggles hissed, springing out as if he'd been shot out of a catapult. He looked back at me with his own special brand of cat-like contempt as he pranced back into the house, no doubt to hack up a revenge hairball on my pillow.

"Well, don't do it again, okay?"

"I swear I'll never do it again." I'd have to find another place to play bomb-shelter. A place that didn't automatically lock when it shut.

"Good." My dad nodded, seemingly satisfied with my promise. He bent over at the waist and yanked lightly on one of my braids. "Because I don't think the emergency release latches were designed with cats in mind."

Immediately after remembering my dad's words I felt around with my fingertips, growing more and more frustrated with my bound hands.

I didn't know where I was being taken, but I knew my time was limited, and if I didn't act now, I'd end up on the wrong end of whatever plans had been made for me by whatever psycho was stupid enough to abduct me.

Preppy would find this asshole, and he'd stop at nothing to make sure he paid. That thought fueled me as I continued my search. My frustration grew. I flipped over onto my stomach and shoved my fingers down as far as they could go into the crease on the floor lining the backside of the trunk. I gasped with delight through my gag when my fingers hit something plastic. I grunted, reaching down further and further until I was finally able to fit my fingers through the loop.

It was now or never.

With my hand and feet bound I was going to have to roll out of the trunk. It was possible I could be hit by another car or die on impact. I pushed that thought aside and again focused my attention on the only two people in the world who mattered.

I tugged on the loop with all my might.

Nothing happened at first, but when I tried again, pulling and tugging until I felt a blood vessel pop in my neck, the roof above me finally lifted. The warm wind flew in and all around me, blowing my hair into my face. The sultry night air instantly beaded up on my skin.

There was no time to count to ten. No time to think of the consequences. An open trunk wasn't something that would go unnoticed.

And it didn't.

The car came to a screeching halt while I was mid-roll, positioned over the rim between bumper and trunk. I went flying into the air, spinning several times over. The flesh on my arms and legs felt as if they were on fire, burning as my skin made contact with the road, dragging against the sharp shell embedded in the asphalt.

When I finally came to a stop, brake lights filled my blurry vision. I heard a car door open followed by the sound of steps on the pavement growing closer and closer.

Dre's told you about me," I called over my shoulder as he followed us across the yard to the driveway.

"She's told me enough, son, and I don't care. I don't care about any of it," he paused. "Just… just go get our girl. Bring her back to me. Whatever it takes."

"Here, take these," Thia said, suddenly appearing with the baby strapped to her chest and Ray beside her. Thia reached into her diaper bag and tossed Bear two pistols with pink handles. "Already loaded," she said. Bear gave both her and the baby a quick kiss on the forehead and jogged over to his bike where he shoved the pistols into his saddlebag.

"Keys," I called to Doe who didn't hesitate to toss them to me.

"I'll watch after Bo," she said with a sad smile.

King and I jumped into Ray's truck as the sound of Bear's bike rumbling to life filled the cab as we took off down the road. I drove while King stuck his head out the passenger seat window, looking at the road for any sign of where Dre might have been taken.

"Do we even know where we're going?" King asked.

"No, but whoever took her couldn't have gone too far," I said. At the end of the road, Bear pulled up alongside us and pointed left, turning that way. I took off in the other direction, pressing my foot on the gas until it hit the floor.

We'd just rounded the corner when we spotted a car parked in the middle of the street. It sped off as we approached, but then something else caught my attention on the road ahead.

No, not something.

Someone.

I slammed my foot on the brake and yanked the wheel to the

left. The truck flipped over onto its side. King came crashing against me. As the truck skid across the road, I wasn't thinking about the metal twisting and crumbling in all around us. My thoughts were on the piles of black hair and pale skin lying in a heap the middle of the road.

I just hoped I hadn't turned too late.

CHAPTER TWO

PREPPY

"**W**ELL FRIENDS," I started, leaning against the wall in King's shop. "This is the fun part of the evening where we get to meet and discuss who's trying to fuck with us and all the ways they need to die." I unsheathed the knife strapped to my belt and began cleaning it with a rag although it was already spotless and I could see my reflection in the blade.

Dre was passed out upstairs. She was scraped up, but nothing was broken. She'd be okay.

Thank fucking God she'd be okay.

Bear sat on the rolling stool King used when he was tattooing. He shook an errant hair from his eyes and made a steeple with his hands, leaning forward with his elbows resting on his knees. "I've always said that the best way to eliminate an unknown threat, is to start by taking out the known ones," he said in his serious biker voice. The same one he used with his brothers when the shit hit the fan.

"So let's make a list," King suggested. His massive frame took up every available inch of the leather sofa. His knees spread wide apart. "Anyone who even has even a little reason to want to cause us or our families harm."

"Then what?" I asked, my head still pounding. I pinched the

bridge of my nose.

Bear shrugged. "Then we kill everyone on it."

"Agreed," King said, crossing his arms over his chest. "By removing all of the threats against us, no matter what the reason. Chances are that we'd also remove the one who tried to get to Dre."

"Process of elimination," I said, rolling the idea around in my head, liking it more and more as it took hold in my brain. "Although, I don't think mass murder is how that process usually starts."

Bear snickered.

"Dre doesn't have anyone after her, so this is definitely something related to me," I said.

"What about that other guy Dre was with when you first met her?" King asked. "The one you didn't kill."

"Eric," I said, hating the way his name sounded out loud. "Before Dre even left the first time I tracked him down, but I was too late. Fucker was already dead."

"Good," King said. "So he's out. Who else?"

Bear cleared his throat. "We finally got a location on the coroner who signed off on your death certificate. There's no way he wasn't on Chop's payroll. Plus, the bitch ran shortly after the news that you were alive started to make the rounds through town. He thought he could hide from us, but he thought wrong. Smoke tagged him in a public housing complex in Fort Romig, just a thirty minute ride down the coast."

"Close enough to make him a suspect for last night too," I pointed out.

King sneered and cracked his knuckles. "Motherfucker should have run further."

I nodded. "He's on the list."

"The guy at the funeral home who was covering for Chop, who told us that open casket wasn't an option because of some shit about an embalming mishap? He's been taken care of courtesy of Jake Dunn," King said, toying with a buckle on one of the leather belts wrapped around his forearms.

"Thank fuck for that crazy son of a bitch," I said, taking a swig of whiskey from the bottle and wiping my mouth with the back of my hand.

"Who else?" Bear asked. "What about Bo's mom?"

"Dre is his mom," I corrected with more bite than I meant to.

"You know what I mean, Prep. His biological mom. The bitch who shot him out her pussy," Bear amended.

"She's dead."

"You?" King asked, asking if I was the one who killed her.

I shook my head. "Nope. Although, it would have been. I gave her enough H to do the job after she signed the adoption papers. The bitch must have had a tolerance like a pre-Iron Man Robert Downey Jr. Anyway, she must have pissed off one of her dealers real good 'cause the fucker put an ax through her head."

"Ouch," Bear said, but the fucker was smiling.

"Yeah, and I thought I had a headache," I said with a laugh. "Where are we with the hospital staff?"

"The hospital shit's a fucking mess," King scoffed. "The staff there signs off on each other's charts. The doctor who was in charge of the ER at the time died a while back of a stroke. Then we found out that the person who comes out to tell you that your loved one is dead isn't necessarily the one who handles the case either. They're understaffed and overworked, so they just get whoever is available to do something. It's been a fucking disaster to sort through. The paperwork leads you in a circle and back to nowhere fast."

"One of my guys is banging the head nurse on the night shift," Bear said. "He's gonna see what else he might be able to get."

I lit a cigarette. "The doctor with that pussy ass smile tattoo on his hand. Dr. Reid. There's no way that fucker's not involved with Chop. Might be trying to get to Preppy through Dre to cover up all the shit he's done. He'd have to have balls the size of tires to attempt it, but it's still a possibility. We've been tracking him for months with no luck. He quit the hospital and vanished, but we'll find him. He'll surface. They always do," I said.

"There's no telling who else there could be involved. That's what's been tripping us up. King lit a joint. "We can't be sure we get to who all was involved unless we take out the entire hospital staff," he laughed, passing the joint to Bear.

"Well, if we," I started, but Bear interrupted before I had the chance to utter a word. "No, Preppy, that's not a fucking option."

I sighed. "I know, but you gotta understand that I've got this thing hanging over me now. I know this shit will take time, and I know that we'll make sure anyone responsible for all this shit pays and pays big," I paused and looked down to my hands. "And another part of me thinks that if there's any chance that someone inside that place might try and come after Dre again, then I'm calling that psychopath, Rage, and letting her blow that hospital into a million fucking pieces."

"How about we call that Plan B," King offered.

"Deal," I said, rubbing my sore shoulder and cracking my

neck.

"You all right, Prep?" King asked. He'd walked away from the accident with only a scratch above his left eye.

"Yeah, but not all of us had fluffy Preppy cushions to land on," I said. "Who else we got?"

"With Chop, Isaac, and Eli out of the picture, there isn't much," King said, exchanging a look with Bear.

"What?" I asked. "What aren't you telling me?"

Bear cleared his throat. "What about Kevin?"

"What about him?" I clipped.

King shrugged. "We don't know much about him. Guy shows up and claims he's your brother." He took a swig of his beer. "Not saying he's involved in it, 'cause just being your brother, if that's what he is, isn't enough to give him reason to want to get to you or Dre. But we're just listing possibilities, right? 'Cause the kid could be one."

"What's his story, anyway?" Bear asked.

I pinched the bridge of my nose. "Haven't really talked to him much. Been so wrapped up in Dre leaving and then getting her back home. And then making sure we found Bo and keeping him safe. Haven't spoken to Kevin more than a few words, and usually, it's because I'm blowing him off. Last night at the party was the first time I'd seen him in months." I felt an odd sense of guilt start to creep into my brain. "Guess that conversation is long overdue."

"How should we handle it then?" King asked.

"Let me deal with Kevin," I said.

Bear sat up straight. "How? You gonna take him out?"

"No," I answered.

King and Bear both shot me looks that were part sympathy

and part 'he's gotta go.'

I looked between my two friends.

"At least not yet."

CHAPTER THREE

DRE

B RAKES SQUEALED GROWING *louder and louder. A high-pitched scraping noise tore through the night. The smell of burning rubber filled the air.*

I managed to lift my head just in time to see a speeding truck become airborne and flip over onto the driver's side with a loud crunch. Metal scraped against the pavement. Orange sparks popped from underneath the truck as it skidded and scraped its way across the pavement.

Directly toward me.

My eyes shot open. I was disoriented when I found myself in the same room where I'd discovered Preppy was alive. Same pink walls. Same Barbie clock on the wall. Of course, I knew now it was Max's room.

I pulled back the covers, noticing that I was only wearing an oversized button-down shirt and panties.

Why am I here?

I searched my brain for the reason why I was in King and Ray's daughter's room but kept coming up blank. I attempted to stretch my arms over my head with no such luck. Soreness and aches stopped me before I was even able to lift them past my chest.

The fabric of my shirt brushed up against my thigh, and I hissed in pain. I lifted the hem to see a big bandage covering most of my upper thigh all the way to my butt cheek.

Suddenly, my newfound consciousness was flooded with memories from the night before. The room began to spin. A sour taste in the back of my mouth I couldn't seem to swallow down.

There was a reason my dream seemed so real.

It wasn't a dream.

With realization came recognition. The truck. The driver. A weight formed on my chest, crushing me under the possibility that I might have lost him.

Again.

"Nooooooo! Preppy! Noooooooo!" I screamed, feeling my heart breaking bit by bit at just the thought of what could have happened. I jumped to my feet and darted to the door. It opened before I could turn the knob. The most beautiful thing I'd ever seen appeared. The man I thought I'd never see again.

Relief was slow to register. I was still in a state of total panic when I looked Preppy up and down. He was shirtless, cuts and scrapes over his shoulder and left side of his chest. His suspenders were off his shoulders, hanging from his pants on both sides of his thighs. I looked him over from his disheveled hair to his bare feet. His eyes were bloodshot, dark circles sat underneath.

I reached out my hand, half expecting it to go right through him as if he were an apparition. When the warmth of his hand enveloped mine, I closed my eyes tightly and sighed.

"Looking for me, Doc?" Preppy asked. And although his words were said with a small trace of humor, his eyes showed only concern as he looked me over for the third time since he'd opened the door. Preppy wagged his eyebrows then winced. He smoothed a finger over the white butterfly stitch covering a three-inch cut above his right eye.

Relief flooded through me. My knees buckled. Preppy caught me by the shoulders before I could fall, holding me close to his chest. Tears welled up in my eyes, and although I tried, I couldn't find the right words to express to him what I was feeling. I didn't know what I was feeling. All I knew was that I never wanted to let go. "Are you okay?" I asked frantically. "Is Bo okay? Where's Bo?"

Preppy pulled away slightly and tilted my chin up so that my gaze met his amber eyes. "Shhhhh. It's okay. I'm fine. Bo's fine. Ray and Thia took all the kids to the beach for the day. Bear's got a couple of his guys looking out for them just to be safe." He placed my hand on his bare chest almost as if he was confirming to me that he really was there. Then he mirrored me, placing his own hand on my chest over my shirt. That's when I realized why Preppy was bare chested. I was wearing his shirt.

Preppy took a step toward me without releasing me so he could push us into the room. He shut the door behind us.

Apparently, I wasn't the only one who couldn't find the words because we stood there silently for several minutes just feeling each other's hearts beating. "How are you feeling?" Preppy finally asked, guiding me back to the bed. I sat down when I felt the backs of my knees hit the mattress. Preppy towered over me, looking me up and down for injuries. "Did…were you hurt? Did anyone hurt you?" he ground out.

"No. Nothing permanent anyway. Nothing is broken that I know of. I'm fine, just a little sore," I said. "Although this doesn't feel all that pleasant." I lifted Preppy's shirt and peeled the corner off of the bandage on my upper thigh, revealing the gnarly road rash beneath.

"Keep it covered. It'll heal," Preppy said, kneeling in front of me. He set his hands on my knees.

"You made it out of the truck," I said. "You're alive."

"You should know by now, Doc, that even death can't keep a motherfucker down," Preppy said with a devilish smile. He shrugged. "Besides, King's monster body just about crushed me, but then we got all flipped around, and I wound up landing on him. I told that fucker to lay off the protein shakes before his size winds up killing someone. It's a public service, really."

I smiled, still not able to believe that we'd both came out slightly worse for the wear but alive after a night that could have ended so differently and so much more deadly.

Preppy sighed and played with the hem of the shirt on my knees. "I don't really want to talk about this shit right now. I want you to rest, but I gotta ask you, Doc. Did you see who it was?"

I shook my head and looked over at the wall, focusing my attentions on the Cinderella clock over the bathroom door, hoping something would come to me that could help.

"How about a car?" he prompted. "A make or a model?"

I shook my head.

"Color?"

I closed my eyes and searched for the answers to his questions, but I came up blank. "I...I was in the trunk. I popped the emergency latch."

Preppy grimaced but quickly covered it up with a soft smile. "That's...that's good, Doc. Quick thinking. Plus, emergency latches were only put in cars starting in the early 2000's, so that's something to start with. Anything else?"

I thought some more. "The car stopped when the person driving realized the trunk was open. They started to come for me. I heard them, but your lights must have scared them off. Next thing I know your truck is skidding to a halt a few inches from me and I don't remember much after that. I don't even know how I got back here."

"You passed out. Shock," Preppy said. "I carried you back."

"You're not hurt?" I said, pointing to a cut on his chest that was still seeping blood.

Preppy shook his head. "The only thing that would have hurt me is losing you."

"Me too," I said, feeling the tears welling up again. I felt an itch on the back of my neck and went to scratch it, finding some sort of gauze taped to my skin. "What is this?" I asked, scratching over the wrap.

"Don't," Preppy said, gently grabbing my wrist, pressing a soft kiss to my knuckles. "It's just a cut. You needed a few stitches is all. You don't wanna rip them out. Stitches suck a lot more when you're conscious." He set my hand down on the bed and laced his fingers with mine, and I felt myself relax, my shoulders fell, and my guard came tumbling down.

Preppy stroked my arm as he talked, trailing his fingers up and down my skin. "Thought I lost you." He laughed, but it didn't reach his eyes. "Again."

"Nah. Can't get rid of me that easily," I said, leaning into his touch. "Who do you think could have done this?" I asked.

"I was about to ask you the same thing. I talked to King and Bear, and the only thing we can come up with is that Bear's been diving heavily into trying to find out who might have been working with Chop to cover up that I was alive. People in the morgue, coroners, doctors, nurses. Shit, even the people at the funeral home."

"So you think it could be someone who thinks Bear's getting too close to the truth?" I asked.

"Maybe, but it still doesn't make sense why they'd come for you and not directly for me. The other theory is that it could just be someone who doesn't like that I'm up and breathing again and wants to get to me through you, although I'm a fairly amazing person so I have no fucking clue who that could be. We're looking into everyone. Including Kevin."

"Your brother?" I asked.

"Let's face it, Doc. He did just kind of come out of nowhere and I still don't really know what he's all about. I'm going to spend some more time with him. Find out what his story is," Preppy said. Preppy's eyebrows turned inward, creases in his forehead deepened. "Dre look. I'm so fucking sorry…"

"No," I interrupted him. "You stop that. I could have lost you too. I can't do that again do you hear me? I can't."

Preppy stood and leaned over me until I was forced to lie back onto the mattress, his hands on both sides of the bed. He looked angry when he said, "I'll never leave you, and you'll never leave me. Is that understood?"

"It is," I said.

The air between us grew thick. I reached out and wiped the blood from the scrape on his chest with my finger. The drop was bigger than I'd thought. It ran down into the lines of my palm, painting the flesh of my hand with his blood.

I glanced back up where the blood had now pooled around one of Preppy's hard nipples. I pressed my thighs together, ignoring the soreness and pain radiating from my legs and focusing instead on the feral way Preppy's nostrils flared as he glanced at his blood on my hand.

He then followed my gaze to his chest.

My skin flushed, and I suddenly felt light-headed.

A shiver ran down my spine.

I reached out to touch him again but pulled back when I realized I was trembling.

"Shit," Preppy swore when he noticed the blood pouring out in a slow but steady stream. He looked from the scratch to me. Neither one of us made a move to clean the blood off ourselves or one another, just continued to stare at one another.

My mouth grew dry.

I couldn't say the same for my panties.

Preppy breathed in deep. A growl erupted from deep within his throat, a sound that made my entire body hum with awareness. He grabbed two fistfuls of my shirt and tore it open, sending buttons careening around the bed and onto the floor.

"That was your shirt," I pointed out, breathing heavily. My face flushed and my cheeks grew hot.

Preppy raked his gaze over my exposed breasts and hardened nipples, and I felt my body come alive under his inspection. "I don't fucking care," he said. "I'd tear every fucking shirt I ever had to shreds for this. I'd walk around shirtless every single day just to see you like this for one fucking second."

Preppy lifted his eyes from my body and our gazes locked.

One heartbeat.

Two.

Then all holy hell broke loose.

Preppy's mouth came crashing down over mine as the dam

built out of concern for one another's well-being broke apart, flooding the air around us with pure unbridled lust. The want and need to feel connected took precedence over everything including breathing. Our tongues collided and tangled. I fisted a handful of his hair and tugged him closer. We couldn't get close enough fast enough.

Not then.

Not *ever*.

Preppy reached around my back and lifted my hips so that my core was flush against his hardness under his pants. I moaned when I felt his heat through the fabric. He grabbed the underside of one of my thighs, kneading it with his hands before forcing my legs around his waist.

We rocked against one another. Writhing. Moaning. Desperate to feel something that wasn't dread or relief.

Alive.

And no one walking the earth had ever made me feel alive the way Preppy did.

I reached between us and unbuttoned his khakis. He pulled his hips back briefly so I could shove his pants and boxers down over the perfect globes of his ass to the floor. He kicked them off his feet and was right back on me where we'd left off. His lips against mine. His cock up against my opening with only the fabric of my panties separating us.

Preppy released my mouth to suck one of my stiffened peaks of my nipple into his mouth, lapping it with his tongue while he dug his fingers into the cheeks of my ass. I writhed against him until I swore if he kept going I could've come just from the friction of his cock against my panties.

"Fuck this, I need you, Doc. I need you now," Preppy demanded. His voice deep and hoarse. He didn't bother taking off my panties. There was no time for that. We were frantic with need. He hooked two fingers around the soaking wet fabric and pulled it to the side as he lined up the massive head of his cock with my pussy. The feeling of the hot silky skin of his hardness right at the place I needed him most sent a wave of pleasure coursing through my body.

I shivered.

"Yes. Now. I need you NOW," I said, my insides contracting around emptiness, desperate to be filled.

Preppy fisted his cock. He moved so quick that by the time he was surging forward, his lips were already back on mine. His tongue seeking mine as his cock sought a different kind of entrance, stretching and filling me each glorious inch by inch until I was incoherently moaning his name into his mouth, rolling my hips to accommodate more of his massive size. Each movement of my body eliciting another spark of need.

Pleasure so great it fucking hurt. A beautiful kind of pain I never wanted to stop feeling.

"Fuck," Preppy groaned, pulling his lips from mine to look down to where we were connected. He pulled out slightly only to surge back in. Harder. Deeper. "Goddamn it, Dre. So fucking good. Every fucking time." He pulled back again and pushed his hips forward, mumbling swears while he repeated this motion until he fully seated himself inside me. The sweet stretching sensation caused my inner walls to tighten around his shaft. We both gasped at the sensation.

The cut on his chest hadn't stopped bleeding, only now the blood started dripping off his nipple onto my stomach. The friction of our bodies rubbing against one another loosened the bandage on my thigh, smearing fresh pink against Preppy's hands and forearms as he used my body as leverage. His own blood dripped steadily from his nipple with each hard thrust, splattering against my breasts, painting my pale skin in a tattoo of red swirls and smears.

We didn't stop.

We couldn't stop.

Shit, a train could've derailed and careened through the fucking window, and we still would have kept going. Maybe because in a way, Preppy and I were our own train. And if we were going to derail, we were going to do it together, connected, with each other's names on our lips.

His thrusts became even more powerful. More demanding.

So did his words.

"You're never leaving me. Say it. You're never fucking leaving me," Preppy ground out.

I wanted to say the words back, but I was literally being fucked senseless. I began to see stars. Brief flashes of white light as he fucked the words into my heart the same way he was fucking my pussy.

Passionate. Relentless. Rough. Frenzied.

We were all of that and more.

So much more.

Preppy pushed my arms up over my head and held my wrists together as he brutally pounded me with his monster cock. Over and over again he punished me and pleasured me. Keeping me on the brink of ecstasy.

I barely registered the pain shooting from my lower back when I lifted my hips to meet his strokes. Our fucking had become wild and reckless. Any sort of rhythm fell by the wayside as we raced down a path where only primal, raw FUCKING would do.

Faster and faster he fucked me. Each push in and pull out resulted in an excruciating amount of pure pleasure coursing through me. I screamed out his name when it became too much and not enough all at the same time. "Preppy. Preppy!" With each use of his name, my cries became louder and louder until I was sure I was screaming in his ear.

"Don't ever fucking leave me!" Preppy repeated. "Look at me, Doc, watch me come for you."

As if I could tear my eyes away from him. There was a beauty in the way the cords of his neck tightened. The way his teeth gnashed together. There was a beauty in him.

Preppy's cock throbbed inside me, and I moaned long and loud as he stroked the sensitive spot on the front side of my inner walls over and over again. His lips parted. The muscles in his shoulders and biceps strained. Sweat beaded on his forehead, running from his temple down the colorful tattoos adorning his neck.

He kept his gaze locked on mine and didn't so much as blink as he came, groaning my name through his release, spurting hot streams of his release within me. Making me his all over again.

I opened my mouth to try and tell him the words he'd wanted to hear, that I was never going to leave, but I couldn't because his final thrust triggered my own orgasm, interrupting any coherent thoughts I might have had, sending me into a twisting tailspin of pure pleasure.

I arched my back off the bed, dug my fingers into Preppy's perfect ass, and shamelessly ground myself against him, riding out the jolts of blinding bliss that left me shaking from the magnitude and force of which I came.

When I could focus again, I opened my eyes and noticed Preppy's head resting against my chest. His arms around my waist. I ran my hand through his hair and down the side of his face and was surprised when I felt wetness on my fingertips.

Preppy glanced up at me, a tear stain on his one cheek, the blood from my chest smeared across the other.

I coughed when my heart skipped a beat, shocked by an electrical jolt of awareness and emotion. I grabbed his face in my hands and finally responded to his earlier demand. "Samuel Clearwater, I promise I'll never leave you," I whispered, my voice as shaky as my limbs. "I love you."

Preppy closed his eyes. A lazy, satisfied smile appeared on his face. He dropped his head back onto my chest. "Love doesn't even begin to cover it, Doc," Preppy said, followed by a yawn.

My heart swelled in my chest. I smiled dreamily and continued to run my hands through Preppy's hair until we both drifted off.

We slept late into the morning and would have slept even later if we hadn't been woken up by the sound of a gun blast.

CHAPTER FOUR

PREPPY

"**S**HIT!" DRE SHOUTED, leaping from the bed. I was thrown from her body, which I was using as the most comfortable pillow I'd ever had the pleasure of sleeping on, falling ungracefully to the floor in a flailing pile of my own naked limbs. "You want it rough, baby you got it," I mumbled, still half asleep.

"What?" Dre asked.

I opened my eyes and found myself staring into my woman's beautiful dark gaze, which looked very confused. "What exactly is going on? You trying to beat me up in my sleep? 'Cause that hardly seems fair," I said groggily, rubbing my eyes and appreciating the fact that Dre was crouched on the floor naked, her pert little ass in the air, still covered in streaks of blood which were now dry. A beautiful reminder of how we'd spent our time before passing out from exhaustion.

"I think someone's firing out there," Dre whispered, crouching down behind the bed next to me. A familiar boom came from outside the window. "See! That sound. There it is again."

"Nobody's firing at us," I said, pulling my woman across my lap. I stood up, dragged her up with me. I positioned her so she could see out of the window down to the driveway below where the very old brown beater I expected to see came rolling up the driveway. The booming sounded again, this time a small poof of fire and smoke from the exhaust pipe accompanied it.

Dre's shoulders instantly relaxed. "Who is that?" she asked, standing on her tiptoes to get a better look.

I stood behind her admiring her ass and shapely legs. Realizing I hadn't answered her she went to turn around to face me, but I pinned her in place, wrapping my arms around her waist and settling my chin on her shoulder. I pointed to the driver's side door, which had just opened. "That," I said. "Is called a piece of shit car." Kevin got out and lit a cigarette. "And that, as you already know, is my little brother."

"Why is he here?"

"I called him. He's been hinting about wanting to work for me," I told her. "So I told him to meet me here."

Dre turned in my arms and raised her eyebrow at me.

"There's no better time than the present to figure out if your family is out to kill your wife," I explained. "Might as well get it over with now."

Before we get too close.

"So, what exactly do you plan on doing?" Dre asked like she knew there had to be more to the story. And she was very right. There was. She wrapped her arms around my neck and nuzzled her nose into my chest. My cock, all too aware of her naked thighs lightly brushing against him, began to jump to attention.

Dre looked down between us to my fully hard cock. She licked her lips and shot me a questioning look. "Don't blame me. When you walk by the family dog and pat him behind the ears he's going to lift his head for attention."

Dre laughed followed by a squeal when I bent over and

picked her up by the waist, tossing her back onto the bed. Her tits bounced as she settled into the pillows. I crawled up onto the bed and in one quick motion flipped her onto her stomach. I ran my hand down her back to the crack of her ass and back up again.

"So," she said, her cheeks reddening when I dipped my fingers even lower into the crease. "You didn't answer my question."

"What question?" I asked, focused on her glistening pussy, already wet for me.

"Kevin. You want to learn more about him. You invited him here. I asked you what exactly you planned on doing with him," she finished. I smacked her ass cheek and she dropped her head, groaning into the pillow.

"Kevin wants in on the family business," I said, tracing the red mark I'd just made on her perfect ass. She glanced over her shoulder and I flashed her a sly smile. "So I'm gonna show him the family business."

I pushed her thighs apart with my knee and fisted my cock, pushing into her tight wet heat. "But Kevin can wait," I groaned, my eyes practically crossing at how good her pussy felt wrapped around me. "There's something else I have to do first."

"Oh yeah?" she asked, pushing back against me. I could practically feel her smile in her voice. "What would that be?"

I thrust hard, pushing my hips forward until I was buried inside of her magical pussy as deep as her body would allow. "You."

A HALF AN HOUR later I emerged from the house and gave

running high-fives to The LAWLESS MC bikers standing guard on each side of the doorway. I hopped down the porch steps three at a time to meet Kevin.

"You've got blood on your neck," Kevin pointed out.

I shrugged and made no point to wipe it off. My inner schoolboy was dying to divulge every single detail of the fuck-fest Dre and I had ourselves that morning to Kevin. However, my inner adult, which I didn't know I had until recently, quickly reminded me that Dre was my wife. A feeling of possession like I'd never known took over. MINE. MINE. MINE. Ran across my brain like a stock market ticker. Shouty-caps and all.

I scowled at Kevin as if he had been standing there watching us fuck or could somehow see her naked inside of my brain.

"Uh, you sure you want to do this today?" Kevin asked, shoving his hands inside the pockets of his board shorts. "I mean, after all that went down last night."

I twirled my keys in my hand. "Listen man, life is short. Nobody knows that better than me. We gotta seize the day. Carpe the diem while we still have diem's to carpe and all that shit." I waved my hand around in the air. "Besides, got the bikers keeping an eye on the family, so all is good for now. We won't be too long." I looked up to the window on the third story and caught a curtain of shining black hair wrapped in a sheet turning away from the window.

"She's fucking hot, dude," Kevin said, staring up at the same empty window.

"She is," I agreed, slapping him on the back and digging my fingers roughly into his shoulder as I led him over to Bear's van. "Touch her and I'll slice both your fucking hands off. Mmm...kay?"

"LEAVE THE PIECES when you goooooo," I sang, tapping my foot to The Wreckers song in my head as Kevin and I stood outside the van in an empty field just outside of town.

"What exactly are we doing out here?" Kevin asked. "I thought you were going to take me to the granny houses. Show me the ropes. You know, how to grow and collect. That kind of thing."

I clucked my tongue. "Oh no, dear brother. Before you become the chef you gotta wash a lot of fucking dishes." Just then a truck hauling a trailer rounded the corner and came barreling through the center of the field, bouncing from side to side as it drove over rock and uneven earth. "You sure you still want in?"

"Yeah," Kevin answered. "What is that?"

"The fucking dishes."

At first glance it looked like any other truck hauling a trailer, complete with the same annoying beeping noise as it backed up into place, finally stopping when the engine was killed.

Jake Dunn, the fucking blonde devil himself, hopped down from the driver's side and rounded the back of the trailer. Ignoring our presence as he unlatched the door. I pulled Kevin aside to avoid being hit by the falling door as it slammed down so hard onto the grass a puff of dirt ascended into the air.

"Whoa, what is all this?" Kevin asked, staring into the trailer.

Inside was an all-metal, very sterile-looking interior. Rows of sharp tools hung from hooks lining the wall. Knives, what looked like machetes, along with icepick looking things and a few hoses. A matching table sat directly in the middle, a drain on one end. A small sink was attached to the wall directly behind the driver's seat.

I extended my arm like a *Price is Right* model. "This is what they call a mobile slaughterhouse, kemosabe," I informed Kevin, lighting a cigarette. "And that fine blonde gentleman is Jake. Since we are here to learn, lesson number one is don't tell Jake he looks like he used to be in a boy band, or fell out of a Teen Beat magazine, or anything else that would make him seem less like the bad-ass motherfucker he is."

Jake scowled, but his blue eyes gleamed.

The guy was a walking contradiction.

I put my arm around Kevin. "Let's change that. Lesson number one is don't talk to Jake. Like EVER," I said. I tipped my chin to Jake. "Morning, Sunshine!" I shouted, ignoring my own rule.

Jake grunted. "Who the fuck is this?"

"Didn't you know? It's bring your little brother-you-didn't-know-about-until-recently to work day."

Jake looked Kevin over like he hated his very existence. He probably did. Because he was Jake. No explanation needed.

"Lesson number two," I said, passing my lighter to Kevin who lit his own smoke. I looked down to his shorts. "Dress for the job you want, not the job you have."

"What exactly does that mean?" Kevin asked, looking at his stained and wrinkled CORAL PINES tie-died T-shirt and flip-flops like there was nothing wrong with what he was wearing.

"It means no more swim trunks unless you're going to pick up chicks at the beach. You dress like a college kid on laundry day. Have some pride, kid."

Kevin huffed. "How am I supposed to dress for the job I want when I don't know what the job is I have, or even what we're doing?" Kevin asked, sounding frustrated.

"I told you," I said as Bear and King pulled up in King's old truck. "You're washing dishes."

King and Bear rounded the back of the truck and lowered the tailgate. Together they each took one end of something about six feet in length, wrapped in garbage bags and rope. They carried him...I mean IT, over to the trailer, setting it on the table with a hard thud. "You want us to stay and help?" King asked, tipping his chin to Jake who was leaning against the table with his legs crossed at the ankles and his arms crossed over his chest.

"Thanks, but we got this, Boss Man," I answered.

King and Bear both looked at the two of us skeptically, the same look they'd given me when I told them what my plans were for young Kevin that day. "Good, gotta go help this asshole we know move anyway," Bear said.

"Yeah, and the guy is skipping out on his own moving day. Can you believe that shit?" King asked. Bear shook his head and I sent them a middle finger salute as they drove away.

"Ummm...what the hell is that?" Kevin asked, looking at the table in the trailer.

"Manure," I answered.

"Really?"

"No. Not really," I sighed. "It's a body-shaped plastic bag, Kevin. What the fuck do you think it is?" I snapped my fingers in front of his face to get his attention. "Now listen up, Danielson."

"Who is it?" Kevin asked, entirely too focused on what was going on in the trailer. His gaze followed Jake's every move as he sharpened one of the knives from the wall with a steel sharpener.

"The dead have no names," I said.

"That's a line from *Game of Thrones*," Kevin pointed out.

"That doesn't mean it's not true."

Jake motioned to the door and Kevin and I lifted it together, holding it up until we heard the click from the inside locking it in place.

"Now what happens?" Kevin asked.

I lit a cigarette and passed it to him then lit another for myself. "Now we wait." We leaned back against the trailer.

"What's this thing used for anyway?" Kevin asked, looking over his shoulder at the closed door of the trailer.

"Well, when Jake here isn't using it for more nefarious purposes, it's usually used as a way for farmers to 'dispatch' their livestock without having to pay hauling fees to have the animals shipped to a facility and then shipped back in sellable pieces."

"Dispatched?" Kevin scratched his clean-shaven chin.

"Yeah, I heard it on the traveling network," I said. "When the host of this show doesn't want to say things like 'brutally slit their throats until all the blood drains out' he says things like 'dispatched'. It makes murdering our food sound a lot more pleasant don't you think?"

"What's he doing in there?" Kevin asked. I didn't know all that much about him, we'd only spoken a few brief times. But I knew the kid wasn't stupid. He might have asked what Jake was about to do but something told me he already knew the answer.

The sound of a buzz saw vibrated within the trailer, followed by a splattering of something against the door. I leaned against it sideways, turning to face Kevin. "Genius isn't it?" I winked.

Kevin watched the trailer as if the goings on inside were being projected onto the door and he could see it all going down. I realized then that although his eyes were wide, it wasn't in horror.

It was in fascination.

Score one for baby bro.

"Looks like you passed the first test. For a second there I was worried how you might react," I said. Just then Jake pounded on the door, three quick raps from within.

We stepped out of the way and let the door fall back down to the ground. Kevin on one side and me on the other.

When Jake appeared again he wasn't wearing a shirt. A black rubber apron was tied around his neck and waist. It was so long it covered the tops of his boots. You wouldn't know the shiny liquid splattered on it was blood unless you looked past Jake and into the scene he'd left behind in the trailer. Different shades of red were dripping from every surface and was splattered across every wall and tool.

"You see, civilians have this thing about death. I think it's all the blood, guts, and gore that bothers them." I waved my cigarette in the air. "Things that hatred and revenge have a tendency to wash away with time. Things like a sense of right and wrong. Guilt. All that bullshit."

Kevin squared his shoulders. "I'm not a civilian," he argued.

"Oh yeah?" I cocked my head to the side. "Then what exactly are you?"

He shrugged then looked as if he was thinking. His eyes met mine. "I'm a Clearwater."

I couldn't come up with a response because for some reason his words rendered me stupid. Thankfully Jake interrupted by stomping down the door. Lighting a cigarette, he rolled his shoulders. His neck cracked with an audible pop. He pointed to the cooler at his feet. "All yours," he said with a faint hint of a smile.

"You want to take a ride with us man?" I asked, Kevin picked up one side of the cooler and set it right back down when he realized how heavy it was.

Jake's eyes lit up with amusement. He shook his head. "Can't. My kids got a ballet recital at four."

"Got ya. Mine wants to sign up for MMA," I told Jake. I couldn't help but to smile as I remembered how Bo had pointed from the fight on the TV and then to himself about a thousand times while jumping up and down. Jake looked at me as if I'd sprouted a dick on the middle of my forehead. "Long story. I'll tell you all about it over a body sometime."

I used to not get how Jake could go from virtual serial-killer type by day to doting family man at night. That was until I had a family of my own and now I respected the hell out of him for it.

Growing up Grace had always told me that you can be a bad boy and still be a good man. I think I was finally understanding what that meant.

Jake turned on a hose and started to wash out the interior of the trailer. Red tinged water sloshed into the drain and over the back of the truck in a mini bloody waterfall. He whistled-as-he-worked like a fucked up eighth dwarf.

Kevin's cheeks turned pink and then red, straining under the weight of the cooler as I helped take it over to the van and set it inside on garbage bags I'd already had laid out.

I slid the door shut. "Now what?" Kevin asked.

I smiled. "Now? Now we have some fucking fun."

Twenty minutes later we were on Billy's old airboat, flying

through the swamp. I switched my theme song from "Leave the Pieces" to "Piece of Me" by Britney Spears.

I had a little bit of a theme going on that day.

We stopped at my favorite spot. Well, my favorite spot for the kind of activity we were doing. It was a clearing next to a sand bar behind a wall of trees where the swamp met the river. Right behind an island King and I had dubbed Motherfucker Island back when we were kids.

Kevin was helping me feed pieces of whoever had been in the bag (The MC's deal, not mine) to the alligators surrounding the boat. "Well, kid. You wanted in," I said. "Now you're in."

Kevin sent a chunk of what I think was a knee sailing into the brush. A splash of commotion erupted as the gators fought over their dinner of human flesh and cartilage. Kevin laughed and set his feet on the edge of the airboat. The sun began to set. "Thanks, Preppy," he said, wiping his hands on his shorts.

I nodded and tipped over the cooler, letting any excess blood drip into the water. I set it back down and clapped a hand over Kevin's shoulder. I smiled brightly. "Welcome to the motherfucking family business, kid."

"Speaking of family," I said. "We haven't exactly got around to talking about that. You ever gonna tell me how exactly you think I'm your brother?"

"Not much to tell," Kevin said, sitting on the edge of the boat with his back to the gator infested waters. "I was born up North. A little town outside Daytona to the same woman who pushed you out."

"So she told you about me?" I asked. "'Cause I find it hard to believe that the woman who left me behind like a couch she didn't want to bother moving actually spoke my name after she bolted."

Kevin shook his head. "Nah, never uttered a word about you. I actually don't remember her speaking at all. A cop found me wandering around the highway in my diaper when I was just a toddler. They handed me over to social services. I grew up in the system."

"Believe it or not that makes you the luckier one of the two of us," I said.

Kevin blew out a breath and rolled his eyes. He paused his beer inches from his lips. "Sure, if you call getting beat by your foster parents lucky. Or not getting fed because I wasn't one of their 'real kids' or maybe lucky was that time I was so desperate I let a trucker jack me off outside of a diner in exchange for a hot meal."

I felt for the kid. I really did but I couldn't help the way my thoughts worked or the burst of laughter that bubbled up and erupted from my mouth.

"You think that's fucking funny?" Kevin said, standing up and rocking the boat from one side to the other.

"Yeah, actually I do."

"Why?" Kevin asked, looking horrified and extremely pissed off. His fists balled at his sides.

"Sit down," I ordered. Kevin huffed as he took a seat, his arms crossed protectively over his chest.

I leaned forward and rested my elbows on my knees. "You want to know why I think it's funny?" I asked, no trace of jokes for this conversation.

"Enlighten me," Kevin snapped.

"Because I would have killed to trade places with you. You think getting a handy from a trucker is a bad deal? Please, I'd trade a dozen fucking truckers jerking my dick." I leaned in closer. "Anything would have been better than getting raped by your stepdad. Better than being left behind like unwanted furniture when your mom moves and leaves you alone with a fucking pedophile."

Kevin's mouth opened and then shut. He scratched at his unruly head of hair. "So what happened to the stepdad."

"He died in a tragic on-purpose accident."

"You killed him?"

"King did," I said. I stood and pointed to the gators encircling the boat. "First notch on his gun belt. That's how we first found out about this spot."

"Shit, man," Kevin said, rubbing his eyes. "I'm sorry I didn't think...."

"So my childhood was a little more rapey than yours. I'm over it, let's move on." I waved him off. "So how the hell did you end up in Logan's Beach?" I asked, reaching into the cooler, the one not designated for body parts. I pulled out two beers and tossed him one.

"I came to find you," Kevin said.

"And?"

"And you were dead," Kevin said. His eyes looking everywhere but mine as he took a long pull of his beer. I did the same. We finished at the same time, crashed the cans against our thighs and wiped our mouths with the back of our hands.

We both laughed when we caught each other going through the same motions and that's when I started to notice the similarities between us. His hair was the only major difference. It was a few shades darker than my sandy blonde. A thick mess on top of his head, several weeks over needing a haircut, but he had the same shape face I did although mine was covered with an exceptionally sculpted beard. We had the same hazel colored eyes although mine were set apart wider. He was even about the same height as I was except my build was much bulkier after having started working out with King several months earlier.

King had called it my, 'gonna get my bitch back' workout routine. Now it was kind of our daily thing.

Kevin popped another beer and tossed me one. "I'd actually only found out about you because when I turned eighteen, foster care was kicking me out. I didn't have nowhere to go. My social worker did some digging, told me I might have a brother. Got your name and possible location. Nothing else." He looked up at me. "Did you know that you're kind of famous around here?"

"Infamous is more like it," I offered.

"Whatever you want to call it. Alls I know is that every single person I talked to knew you or knew of you. I even looked up your mug shot so I could see what you looked like. I drove by your house a time or two to see where you lived, before I heard you kicked it. Visited your grave once. Brought you a beer." He chewed on his lip. "Well, I *brought* you a beer. I might have drank it for you."

I smiled. "How fucking thoughtful of you."

"I met Meryl and Fred when I was selling weed by the bus station. Nice guys. Let me crash with them a few times but they're not around much. I tell you what though, when you showed up at their house that day, running from that cop I nearly pissed myself when I realized it was you."

I held up my index and thumb and looked at him through the small space between. "It was a bit shocking for me as well. Never expected to have anyone call me their brother," I said. "Is your last name really Clearwater?" I asked, remembering what he'd said earlier.

Kevin shook his head. "No," he said like he couldn't believe what he was about to say. "It's Schmooter."

I laughed and toasted Kevin and his ridiculous last name, clinking my beer to his. "You need a nickname or something," I said.

"Yeah, I think you're right," he agreed.

"I'll come up with one for you...Schmooty?"

Kevin shook his head.

I started up the boat. "The Kev-ster? It's very *Home Alone*. Very 1990."

He rolled his eyes.

I threw down the throttle and shouted over the wind. "Handy-Kevin?"

Kevin flicked me off.

"What? Too soon?" I asked.

"Fuck off," Kevin said, trying to hide his smile with his hand.

"I hate to bring this up when we're having such a swell time and all," I started, raising my voice above the sound of the engine and the wind as I sped us up faster and faster. Kevin gripped the metal bar attached to the seat between his legs. "But you know if I find out you had anything to do with what happened with Dre last night, or if you fuck with her or my kid in any way that makes me twitchy, you'll be the one getting fed to the those fucking gators on the next go-round."

I don't know how I expected him to react after I threatened him, but I didn't expect him to smile, which was exactly what he did. "I didn't doubt that for a second, Prep," he shouted back.

"I'm glad we're on the same page."

I pushed down the throttle, zooming over the shallow water and tall grass. I made a few sharp turns and a few one-eighties for shits and giggles along the way. Kevin even sang along with me for a very off pitch rendition of "Piece by Piece" by Kelly Clarkson. Well, it was more 'screaming into the wind' than actual singing.

In my gut, I didn't feel like Kevin had anything to do with trying to take Dre, but I couldn't be a hundred percent sure. At least not yet. And family to me was everything, but the saying that blood was thicker than water didn't mean jack shit to me because I knew who my family was and blood was something we spilled for one another, not shared.

"Maybe next time we come out here we'll run the gators. See how big your balls are," I said.

"What the hell is run the gators?" Kevin asked.

"I'll show you next time," I said.

After I few minutes of silence I looked over to Kevin and burst out laughing. His mouth was wide open, his cheeks puffed out by the wind, exposing all this teeth and gums. He gave me a thumbs up.

Silly little fucker.

I kind of like my brother. I thought to myself.

It would really suck to have to kill him.

CHAPTER FIVE

PREPPY

SIXTEEN YEARS OLD

I WAS BORN MINUTES away from the beach and minutes away from the sticks, in Logan's Beach, Florida. Saltwater in my veins. Dust on my soul.

Which was probably the reason it never bothered me when Bear, King, and I didn't spend our Friday nights like most teenagers in LB were. Kicking up shit in the woods or sneaking beer into the drive-in dollar movie theater.

Then again, King, Bear and I weren't most teenagers.

Our Friday nights were spent a little differently. Like rowing out to an island to bury our 'investments.'

Although it didn't have an official name, we'd dubbed the little five-acre slab of land separating the Bay from the Gulf as Motherfucker Island.

MFI for short.

Motherfucker Island was uninhabited and only about as big as a typical strip mall. Dense brush covered most of it, for the exception of a small clearing in the center made up of red dirt and shell. An almost perfect line of mangroves lined the perimeter.

We'd started our 'supply bunker' a year before. It was really just a hole in the ground, but you could only reach the island by boat and the mangroves and alligator infested shallow waters around it didn't exactly make it a hot-spot destination for anyone but three delinquent teens trying to hide newly acquired cash, guns, and drugs.

The apartment King and I were renting wasn't much by way of security unless you consider the flimsy chain lock on the door with rusted hinges secure. Hence the need for MFI.

The sun was setting as we rowed toward Motherfucker Island in the tiny metal boat barely large enough to hold the three of us. The time of day when it wasn't still day but night had yet to take over the sky. I liked to call it the time of day when I couldn't see shit. The rays from the falling ball of fire in the sky reflected off everything in sight causing me to go half blind as I rowed, hoping King and Bear could keep us on target.

A manatee blew out water a few feet from our boat. "Hey, buddy," I said, leaning over the side and lightly patting the surface of the water.

"What the fuck are you doing?" King asked with a laugh.

"Making him come to me. I saw it on a TV show when I was a kid." I continued to pat the water. "Come here, buddy. Come to Preppy," I said, whistling like I was calling for a dog.

"I'm pretty sure that only works for dolphins," Bear said, a cigarette dangling from his lip.

"Manatees are dolphins much fatter, slower cousins," I argued. I either remembered that fact from somewhere, or made it up.

Chances are I made it up.

The manatee's head disappeared. He flipped his tattered

back fin in the air before disappearing back under the water, creating a circular ripple in the surface where he'd just been.

"Anyone else think the manatee just flipped us off?" King asked.

"He sure as fuck did," Bear agreed. "Way to go dolphin-cousin whisperer."

I sat back up and glared at my friends. "It's your attitudes that scared him off. It deters even the wildlife." I reached for my lighter in my back pocket. "In addition to girls."

"I don't have any problems with the girls," King argued.

"Yeah, they'll fuck you, but they're scared of you," I pointed out.

"Don't bother me none," King said, taking a deep breath. "Prefer it that way, actually."

"This town can be such shit," Bear said, exhaling smoke. He pointed to his cigarette at the disappearing ripple in the water where the manatee had just been. "And then you see shit like that and it makes you think that maybe it's not so fucking bad."

"I fucking love this town," I said. "And we're gonna own it someday. Well on our way."

"Then we're gonna own one of those," King said, tipping his chin to several huge homes on pilings, towering above the water. Some of them were dark, hurricane panels covering the windows and doors. A sure sign that they were owned by someone who only lived in them 'in season' which was somewhere from November to March.

"What a fucking waste," King said, echoing my thoughts. He pointed up to one such house. A three story stilt home sitting almost right under The Causeway. It was completely dark, storm shutters on every window and door. It had a huge backyard with a neglected fire pit, bricks crumbling from the pile.

"Fucking shame," I agreed. "When we get one of those big 'ole fuckers for ourselves I'm never leaving the place. Like a king in his castle."

King shot me a look. "We already got a King."

I knew he was goading me because he had this thing he did when he was trying to be serious but about to crack where the corner of his lip would ever so slightly twitch like he was physically fighting his reaction. "Like a Preppy in his castle then," I amended.

King smiled.

"I'm glad you let that smile out, Boss-Man. I was afraid for a second that you were going to spontaneously combust. That or you had a serious case of constipation," I said.

Bear snorted. "Well, make sure that when y'all get one of them places that you make room for me," Bear said, sounding defeated.

"Uh, Bear. You're in a biker gang," I pointed out. I quit rowing just long enough to pass him the dented Pepsi can I'd made into a temporary bong after dropping my rolling papers into the fucking Caloosahatchee. "I hate to sound all mean-girls on you, but...you can't live with us."

"It's a motorcycle club," Bear corrected, looking off into the distance. "And I ain't moving in. Just make sure you have space for me if I need to crash."

King and I glanced at each other and understanding passed between us that Bear meant he needed a place to crash for when his ol' man, Chop, pushed him to the edge, which he was doing more and more of ever since Bear turned official Prospect for the MC.

"Sure thing, man," King said, casually.

The three of us continued to survey the darkened waste of real estate until we came upon one that was different than the others.

It was lit up and being that it was closer to the water than the others, we could see directly inside to where a family was eating dinner together at the dining room table. A mom, dad, and little boy. They were smiling and laughing together. "Didn't know families actually did that," I said, not realizing how sad it sounded at the time.

"You don't want that," Bear argued. "Shit looks boring as fuck."

King agreed with a slight nod of his head.

"I didn't say I wanted that," I quipped, shrugging my shoulders. "I just didn't know people actually did that. Thought it was made up or something you only see on TV."

"It is," Bear said. "What you just saw there was a lie. The dad is probably fucking his assistant, who's a dude, mom's knocked up by the principle of junior's school and has a thousand dollar a day drug habit, plus junior is so high on ADD meds he doesn't know his dick from a wet noodle."

"I feel like you've given this way more thought than it deserved," I observed as the family eating dinner grew further and further away. "Wait?" I faked a gasp. "Are YOU the one fucking the dad?"

Bear punched me in the shoulder and smiled. "Boring as fuck," he said again, like it was a fact he wanted me to remember. He slid his cigarette to the side of his mouth so he could use both arms to row against the growing current.

"Yeah," I agreed. "Boring as fuck."

As we approached the island everything was cast in shadows, making the long roots of the mangroves look like hundreds of skinny legs dipping into the water. The trees themselves appeared to be large spider-like creatures standing guard around the island.

I held the flashlight, trying to find the clearing we'd hacked out months before. The light caught the yellow glowing eyes of a dozen or so gators lingering at the surface of the water. Some darted under the second they found themselves in the way of the beam, other braver ones slinked toward our boat without creating any sort of wake to better inspect the intruders.

Us.

"It's like a gator orgy out here," I said.

"Yeah, so let's get over there quickly without tipping the goddamned boat before it becomes a gator buffet," King said.

Once we found the clearing we paddled toward it with all of our strength to keep the tide from pushing us back. The second the boat made contact with land King jumped out first pulling the boat further onto the shore, scraping the metal bottom of the boat over the rock and shell.

Bear and I followed, each of us carrying backpacks with our stash. It only took us an hour or so to locate our hole, dig it up again, bury our stash and cover it back up.

As we made it back to the boat my flashlight again caught the yellow eyes of the gators surrounding the boat. One thrashed as it caught a fish in its mouth before diving back under the water with its meal between its teeth. "Great night for a swim," I sang, looking back at King and Bear.

"You afraid?" Bear said, slinging his empty backpack into the boat.

"You're the pussy out of the three of us," I said. "Bet you wouldn't dip your big toe in the water."

Bear raised a brow. "Oh yeah? I'll do you one better, I'll run in, knee deep if you run in with me."

"One lap around the boat?" I asked, already kicking off my shoes and rolling up my pants. Bear did the same. We both looked to King.

"Fuck," he said, tugging off his boots. "The only reason I'm doing it this is so I don't have to fucking hear about it for the rest of my goddamned life." He stood at the edge. "Don't tell Grace a word of this," he muttered.

The three of us stood at the edge and Bear pushed the boat halfway into the water.

"Ready?" I asked, cracking my neck and rolling my shoulders. "First motherfucker to get eaten…well, dies."

"I'm not scared," Bear said.

"Me neither," King chimed in.

"Okay then," I said. "Ready. Set. Goooooo!" I shouted as the three of us splashed through the water like a herd of zebra running from a lion. It only took a few seconds for us to round the boat before we collapsed onto the shore, breathing hard from the adrenaline rush.

"All thirty fingers and toes accounted for?" King huffed.

"Yeah," Bear and I both said at the same time. I held a finger in the air, "But Bear's pinky toe on his right foot is weirdly smaller than the rest of his toes, so the 'all finger and toe' thing is subjective at best."

"Shut the fuck up, Preppy," Bear said, reaching for me to hit me but his fist fell short, smacking the ground instead.

"That wasn't so bad," I said, still gasping for air.

My life would never be like the perfect-looking family eating dinner in that window, but it didn't have to be, because at that moment, with my friends by my side, I decided I'd much rather live the kind of life that had me splashing through gator infested waters, feeling very much ALIVE.

I glanced over to King and Bear who recognized the look on my face and cringed.

"Wanna go again?"

CHAPTER SIX

DRE

AFTER PREPPY LEFT with Kevin I called my dad to reassure him I was okay. He sounded as if he'd been waiting by the phone so it took quite some time to calm him down and put his mind at ease that I was safe, which was hard when I wasn't so sure myself. Apparently, I didn't do that great of a job convincing him because he decided to stay in town for a while. At least until he was sure whatever threat was looming out there was gone.

After we hung up and I promised we'd get together in the next day or so, I realized that in all the confusion over what had happened the night before I'd forgotten a few things. Number one, I didn't get a chance to give Preppy his surprise. The shiny black classic Chrysler was still sitting in the darkened back corner of the parking space under the house, covered with a tarp.

I'd also almost forgot that Mirna's house was now mine again.

Not mine. OURS.

That thought made me smile from ear to ear.

I don't know how Preppy and Ray pulled it off, especially without telling me for so long, but I was beyond grateful they had. That house meant so much to me and I couldn't wait to get back in it. It was like the start of a new life and the rebirth of an old one.

Moving was the perfect distraction I needed to take my mind off the events of the night before. When the rental truck showed up at the house I immediately felt a sense of relief that I could focus on something other than who could be out to get me, although the stinging pain from the wound on my leg and other numerous scrapes and scratches, took the liberty of reminding me every other movement.

Besides one small scrape on the side of his arm you'd never thought that King had been in an accident the night before, never mind one where the truck flipped on it's side. When I thanked him for coming to my rescue, he looked at me as if my thanks were ridiculous, and then him and Bear started loading up everything from the garage apartment into a we-haul rental truck, including the sofa, and the bed, which had already been dismantled. Come to think of it, the bed being in pieces was probably the reason I'd woken up in Max's room that morning.

We didn't have much by way of furniture, but we didn't need it. Thankfully Mirna's house was cozy and it wouldn't take much to fill it up.

Everything else we owned, clothes and all, had already been packed up into boxes so it didn't take long for the boys to get it all onto the truck.

Ray came back from the beach with the kids and when Bo came bounding out of Ray's new SUV I hugged him tight and didn't let go until he started to wiggle in my arms. "Are you okay?" I asked. The sound of him calling for me still echoing in my thoughts. I shook it off, not wanting to pass on any of my worry or fear to him.

Bo nodded and pointed to a scrape on my cheek.

"I'm okay," I said, touching my fingers to the small scab. "It's just a scratch." I took his little hand in mine and we piled back into Ray's car together.

After the ritual of making sure everyone was back in the car and buckled in their boosters and car seats, checking to make sure every buckle was at chest level and every safety latch was tight, we took off for Mirna's.

Home.

Bear and King were already unloading when we arrived. Some of Bear's guys were there as well, standing guard along the perimeter of the yard and at the end of the driveway.

"You remember this place?" I asked Bo as we un-piled all the kids one by one and set them free to run about the yard and house.

Bo nodded enthusiastically.

I crouched down next to him and hugged him close to my side. "Do you want to go pick your room? You can have either the first one on the left, that used to be my old room, or the room at the end of the hall." Before I'd finished my sentence Bo was already up the steps and in the house, darting past King and Bear who were carrying the sofa inside.

It took less than an hour to unload everything. Bear and King checked with the bikers they'd left behind and took off. Ray stuck around for a little while to help put dishes away in the kitchen but it didn't take long for the kids to grow restless.

"Thank you so much for all your help," I said to Ray as we stood outside her SUV after packing all the kids away again. I'd left Bo in his room, the one that used to be the grow room, laying on his back staring at the ceiling fan spin round and round with a goofy grin on his face.

"No problem. Thia's sorry she couldn't help but Trey's got another cold and she didn't want the other kids to get it."

"Tell her not to worry about it and when Trey's feeling better we can have a girl's night."

"Now that's what I'm talking about," Ray said.

"Thanks again, Ray," I said, wrapping her in a tight hug.

"Is this pre or post kiss? Doesn't matter. Either way, I'm very okay with your decision to step outside of our marriage...but only if I can watch." I didn't need to turn around to know that Preppy was standing behind me, but when I did, I was surprised to see Kevin still with him. Especially because Preppy had called to say he was dropping him at his place before meeting me at the house.

Ray got in her SUV and buckled her seatbelt. "I'll see you later," she said to me before turning to Preppy. "For the record, Preppy you showed up post kiss, and you missed it. It was pretty epic. Tongue and everything." Ray stuck out her tongue as she backed out of the driveway. All three kids in the backseat mimicked her, sticking out their tongues as well.

"Can you just lie to me and tell me that really happened?" Preppy asked, wrapping me in his arms. He stared down at my lips. "Never mind. I like the idea of these lips being only mine." He pressed his soft lips to mine then pulled back slightly. "Unless you really did do it in which case..."

I laughed and gave my man a quick kiss. "Hey Kevin," I called over Preppy's shoulder.

"Hey, Dre," Kevin said. He was standing awkwardly by the front porch, looking everywhere but at us, fiddling with the strings on the front of his board shorts.

I stepped out of Preppy's hold, not wanting to make Kevin feel uncomfortable. Preppy reached in his pocket tossed Kevin a set of keys. "Go get your bag from the van," he told him. Kevin nodded and headed down the driveway while we went inside.

We quickly checked in on Bo who was in his new room, still on the floor, playing a game on the tablet Preppy had insisted on buying him. He gave us a smile and a thumbs up. After I closed his door I took Preppy's hand in mine and yanked him into what had been Mirna's room but would now be our master bedroom. I shut the door behind us. "I like where this is going," Preppy said, pulling me flush against his hard chest.

"No," I said, wiggling out of his grasp and walking around to the other side of the bed. I had to put some space between us before Preppy rendered me dumb and I couldn't get my words out.

"No?" Preppy asked, looking a little hurt.

"I just mean not right this second," I corrected. His expression instantly brightened. "Kevin," I prompted. "You were going to take him home, now he's getting his bag from the van."

"Yeah, about that," Preppy said, scratching his neck. I waited for him to continue, but his only answer was an awkward grin.

"After last night I might be a little confused," I explained. "So bear with me. What happened? Why didn't you take Kevin home?"

"I did take him home, that's the fucking problem," Preppy said with a groan. He plopped down on the bed and unlaced his boots, kicking them off he lay back on the mattress and looked at me upside down. I sat down next to him and stroked his hair. "The place where he lives is a shit hole. And I don't mean that like it had a bulb out on the porch or like the espresso machine overflowed and stained the carpet. I mean it like I could smell actual shit from the street. Kevin said the landlady who rents him the room has a fuck ton of cats and no litter boxes. Plus, roof over his room is non-existent. It's covered with a tarp where there was fire damage that was never fixed."

"Shit," I said. "Why does he stay there? Can't he find another place?"

Preppy shook his head. "I asked him that. He said he can't afford anything else. Makes sense though. The kid's only nineteen. Being a small time weed dealer with a ninth grade education doesn't get you too far." He sighed. "I know I should've asked you if I could bring him here, but it was kind of a spur of the moment thing. All I knew was that I couldn't let him stay in that place so I told him to pack his shit and I brought him here." Preppy looked up at me through his ridiculously long lashes. "He can't go back there. I won't let him."

My heart squeezed.

"You mad?" he asked.

I leaned over and pressed an upside down kiss to his lips. "No," I said. "I'm not mad. I'm very proud of you, Samuel Clearwater."

"Thanks, Doc." Preppy nuzzled into my touch as I continued to run my fingers over his hair, lightly scratching along his scalp with my nails.

"Do you trust him?" I asked.

Preppy closed his eyes for a beat. "No. Not entirely, but I still couldn't turn my back on him."

There was a knock at the door. "Uh, Preppy?" A hesitant voice asked from the other side.

"You can come in, Kevin," I called out.

The door slowly opened. Kevin stood there with a tattered army green duffel bag slung over his shoulder. "There's someone here for you. Outside. Some guy."

"Who?" Preppy asked, sitting up and reaching for his boots.

"I'm not sure, but he's kind of being a dick," Kevin said.

I went over to the window and pulled the lacy ivory curtain to the side. I peered out and spotted a man wearing overalls, standing against a large blue unmarked semi truck that was parked in the street. The man was impatiently tapping a clipboard against his leg while glancing between bikers guarding the yard.

"Kevin, Doc, you stay here," Preppy ordered. He opened the door to Bo's room. "Come on my boy. It's here." Bo scrambled to his feet and ran after Preppy who didn't appear to be worried. He had a little spring in his step as he bound toward the front door. He was excited at whatever was waiting for them outside.

"What's going on?" I asked.

"It's a surprise," Preppy called back. The screen door slammed shut behind them.

"A surprise?" I muttered, trying to figure out what kind of surprise was delivered to your house in a semi-truck. "What the hell could it be?"

"I've got no fucking clue," Kevin said, coming to stand beside me at the front window. "But whatever it is, it's making a shit ton of noise in the back of that truck."

"Noise?" I asked, scrunching up my nose. "What kind of noise?"

Kevin shrugged and turned back toward the kitchen.

"The screaming kind."

"YOU GOT HIM a dog?" I asked, spying the leash and dog bed in the hall when Preppy finally said it was safe to come out of our bedroom because he'd insisted I'd hide while he and Bo got 'the surprise' ready.

"Suuuurrreeee..." Preppy said. Just then a loud squeal ripped through the room followed by laughter. A blur of white and black tore into the living room and out to the backyard through a new doggy door that had been installed in the sliding glass door. Bo followed, crawling through the door behind him.

"That wasn't a dog," I stated, walking over to the kitchen window.

"That depends. What's your definition of *dog*?" Preppy asked.

I held up my hands to my chest with my fingers curled over my palms to mimic paws. "Wuff. Wuff."

"Then no. No, I didn't get him a dog. Not in the DNA sense." Preppy said. He stood behind me and wrapped his arms around my waist. He bent his neck and pressed his nose into my hair and breathed in deep, inhaling my scent. I relaxed into him. "You smell so fucking good," he groaned.

"Is that who I think it is?" I asked, still not believing what I was seeing. Bo chasing around a giant pig in the backyard. "That's not just ANY giant pig, is it?" I asked, feeling my hopes start to rise.

Preppy shook his head and smiled into my hair. "Nope. It's not."

"Oscar?" I asked, spinning around in Preppy's arms. "How is that even possible?"

Preppy shrugged. "Mrs. Saddleston, the lady he was placed with after Mirna, died a few weeks ago. The Alzheimer's agency thinks that Oscar was too sad to be placed with another Alzheimer patient, apparently he doesn't handle death well. Anyway, it was time for him to retire and they said he could come back and live with us if we wanted. So…"

"So you got Oscar back!" I shouted, wrapping my arms around his neck and standing on my tiptoes to place a soft kiss on the corner of his upturned lips. "You did it. You got him back!" I said, not sure if I was even making sense I was so excited.

"Yes, ma'am. I motherfucking did it," Preppy said proudly.

"Thank you," I breathed, turning back to the scene in the backyard. The one where my son was playing with his new, my old, pig.

"After all, every boy needs a man's best friend," Preppy said, running his hands across the delicate skin on the front of my throat and across my collarbone.

"I'm pretty sure that they meant dog when they came up with that saying," I replied. My nipples hardened.

"Actually, I'm pretty sure that pussy is a man's best friend. But we'll just have to agree to disagree," Preppy said, dropping his hands to the waistband of my skirt, dipping his fingers inside briefly before pulling them back out. "But just to be sure," he said, reaching down to the hem of my skirt and pulling it up so he had access to my panties. He pushed the fabric aside and teased my wet folds with his thumb. "I'll need to thoroughly investigate."

He inserted one long glorious finger inside of me and just when he reached the point that made me shudder it was gone and Preppy was righting my skirt and maneuvering me so that I was standing in front of him. Presumably to hide the massive erection prodding me in my ass because Bo and Oscar came racing through the door. Bo pointed to the pig and jumped up and down, his face red with excitement. Oscar pushed Bo, nuzzling him in the arm until Bo fell over onto his butt. The smile never leaving his face.

"You know. That's not just any pig, Bo," I said, leaning down to pet Oscar who was actually wagging his curly tail when he saw me. "Hey there, boy."

"No. He's a super pig," Preppy added.

"Yep, he's a super pig," I agreed.

We spent the next couple of hours playing with Oscar who was still as active as ever in his old age and seemed happier than a…well, happier than a pig in shit, to be home again although I did find him lingering in the doorway of Mirna's room at one point. He looked sad when I scratched him on the head and told him that she wasn't coming back. But when Bo came skipping down the hallway, Oscar squealed and happily followed him back out into the yard.

When I turned around from the door Preppy was staring at me with an unreadable expression on his face. "This was a great surprise. Thank you so much," I said as he cornered me in the hall, pressing my back up against the bathroom door.

He pressed a kiss to the tip of my nose and dropped his forehead to mine. "You ain't seen nothing yet, Doc."

CHAPTER SEVEN

DRE

F OR THE NEXT few weeks our little family settled into a
comfortable routine. The bikers continued to stick around
the house to watch over things, but they'd been reduced from
over six of them in the yard at a time to only two. We hadn't
figured out who or why I was a target that night but Preppy told
me it was being handled and I trusted him with his word. I
didn't ask about the details, the where, how's, and why's, because
I know he'd tell me, and sometimes ignorant bliss is just that.

Bliss.

Kevin and Preppy were spending more time together. Preppy
even started taking him to the granny houses to teach him how
to set up a grow room and schmooze the grannies.

We enrolled Bo in a special private school, and although it
was summer he was attending their summer school program part
time so they could evaluate his needs. There were no records of
him ever attending school and he hadn't spoken another word
since he'd yelled for me that night. We didn't know what exactly
he'd suffered at the hands of his mother and stepdad, so Preppy,
drawing on his own childhood traumas, thought it best Bo saw a
professional to make sure he didn't suffer any more emotionally
than he already had, so he was seeing a counselor who specialized

in child abuse twice a week.

If everything went well, which so far it seemed like it was, then Bo would officially be attending kindergarten in the fall. Preppy also hired a private tutor to help Bo learn to communicate better through sign language. The tutor would spend an hour with Bo alone, then Preppy and I would join in on the session and we would all learn together. Kevin eventually joined us and the four of us had a pretty good grasp on the basics.

I spent most of my time when Bo was at school making our home feel like a home, refinishing furniture I'd found in the garage, and fixing broken pipes and wiring. It wasn't a huge space so I painted the walls with a fresh coat of eggshell. The furniture was all white and I'd sanded down the dining room table to give it a worn look. Most importantly I made sure Bo's room was everything a little boy could ever want. When Preppy had asked Bo what theme he wanted for his bedroom he chose cowboys and Indians. Not the most politically correct choice, but we weren't about to explain that to a six-year-old.

I painted the walls of his room and his furniture a pale grey. I bought a scrap of white canvas and found some heavy sticks that I sanded down. I painted grey and orange zig-zag stripes on the canvas and attached them to the smooth sticks, making Bo his very own little tee-pee. I hung a branch that I'd spray painted black from the ceiling and layered it with white twinkling lights. I finished the look with a few fun colored throw pillows I'd sewn patches on. One with red cowboy boots, the other with a yellow cowboy hat and matching bandana.

The end result was a contemporary looking kid's room that was both fun and functional.

I'd just finished setting up a mini table and chairs in the

corner of his room to create a little play/work station when I heard a noise that sounded like shuffling feet on the porch.

I walked out into the living room and heard the noise again, this time right on the other side of the door but no one knocked or rang the bell.

It's probably just Rev or Wolf.

I steeled myself, grabbed the handle, and swung open the door.

I squeaked in surprise to find Preppy standing there with a dazed look on his face, his closed fist in the air like he was about to knock. "I forgot my keys," he said flatly.

"Oh my God, what's wrong?" I asked, fear coursing through me. "I thought you were meeting with King." That's when I realized Preppy didn't look dazed at all.

He looked horrified.

"I think they're trying to kill me," he whispered.

"Who's trying to kill you?" I asked, stepping aside to let Preppy in so he could avoid whatever threat was after him. But then, two shrieking little blonde blurs zipped past us into the house, my knees buckled as they sideswiped my legs on the way in.

Preppy grunted when the little boy elbowed him in the junk.

"Them," Preppy groaned, holding the crotch of his khakis. He pointed to the two little kids who were now chasing each other around the island in the kitchen. "Them. They're the ones trying to kill me."

"Max and Sammy? KIDS!" I slapped him in the arm. "You gave me a fucking heart attack."

Preppy straightened himself and followed me into the house. He stood behind the couch and continued to stare at King and

Doe's two oldest kids as they darted down the hallway. Immediately there was a crashing sound like they'd run into the wall followed by giggles and more running.

"Where is Bo?" Preppy asked.

"Taking a nap in our room, but something tells me that with those two racing around he won't be napping for much longer," I said.

"I don't know where they get all that fucking energy from. Bo's not like that. He plays hard but I never get the feeling that he's out to fucking kill me. These two don't slow down. They don't even breathe. Plus, they keep telling me they're hungry, but they won't eat a damn thing I give them, which was fucking everything," Preppy said, leaning his elbows on the counter and looking up at me through his lashes which were ridiculously long for a man.

"Uncle Preppy we want mac and cheese!" Max said. "And I think Sammy broke your lamp thingy."

"No, we want burgers. Aunt Dre can we have burgers?" Sammy chimed in. "And Maxy broke your lamp, not me. I was being good."

"No Sammy, I want mac and cheeeeeeese," Max argued with her brother, elbowing him in the ribs.

Preppy leaned toward me while the kids continued to argue. "Is it possible for kids to be bi-polar?" he asked as the twosome once again started laughing and chasing each other around the house. "Seriously," Preppy said, snapping me out of my thoughts. "I think they need A.D.D. meds. Or lithium. We got any lithium?" He opened and closed each of the kitchen cabinets.

I rolled my eyes. "Nope," I laughed. "Fresh out, I'm afraid."

Preppy slumped his shoulders in defeat.

I laughed. "They don't need lithium, Preppy, they just need to burn off some energy." I put two fingers in my mouth like my dad taught me to do and whistled loud and long. The kids froze.

"Do you guys kiss and hug like Mommy and Daddy?" Sammy suddenly asked. "Because it's soooooo gross and they do it aaaalllllll the time." The worth gross sounded more like growth with his two missing front teeth.

"Uhhhhh…" I stammered. I felt Preppy's eyes on me. My skin broke out into gooseflesh. I was about to change the subject but Max beat me to it.

"You're real pretty, Aunt Dre," she said, turning at the waist from side to side with her hands behind her back. "Like my mommy."

"So are you," I said, bending down to pull on one of her springy curls. She giggled and my heart seized in my chest. I cleared my throat. "So how about I make you two something to eat while you two go play outside?" I said, opening the sliding glass door. "Don't leave the yard," I called out, but I was already talking to their backs because before I finished speaking they'd already darted into the yard and were again a blur of giggles and shrieks. I kept the glass part of the door open, but shut the screen portion.

"They're such sweet kids," I said, turning back to Preppy who was looking at me with confusion written all over his face.

"They're the fucking devil," Preppy said.

"They're just kids. Don't you remember how you were as a kid?" I opened a cabinet and pulled out a blue box of mac and cheese and started boiling some water.

"I don't think I ever got to be a kid, not like that," he said, watching through the window as Sammy and Max played leapfrog in the backyard. "I think I went straight from baby to amazing adult with no stops in between in holy terror zone."

I pushed my index finger against his chest. "And yet...you never really grew up," I teased.

"Oh you got jokes now?" he asked, tugging on the hem of my shirt.

"Some days." I was about to turn back to the stove when my eyes landed on the thick scar cutting into his skin, slicing several of his colorful tattoos in half with a jagged white line that used to be crimson.

Preppy lifted his arm to look at what had caught my attention and I felt the embarrassment creep up my cheeks. "I didn't mean to stare, it's just that it's all healed now."

"You can stare all you want, Doc," Preppy said, pulling me into his chest. "You can touch all you want too."

A sizzling sound caught our attention. The pot on the stove was boiling over. Foam spilled over the top, landing on the hot burner with an angry hiss. "Fuck," I said, grabbing the pot with two oven mitts. I was about to dump out the water and half cooked noodles when Preppy stopped me.

"Wait," Preppy said. "Set it back down." He turned the dial to the left, lowering the heat of the stove. "Do we have any olive oil?"

I rummaged through a cupboard and found what he needed, tingles shot up my arm when our fingers brushed as he took the bottle of oil from me but it was hard to deny that I felt anything when my nipples were peaking against my shirt. If he looked over there was no way he wouldn't be able to see his effect on me.

Preppy poured a bit of the oil into the pot with the noodles and stirred it. Instantly the rising foam fell back down. "All fixed," he said proudly.

I cleared my throat and wet my dry lips. "Are you going to tell me why you have King and Ray's kids?" I asked curiously, taking a package of ground chuck out of the fridge. Preppy took the package from me and had already washed his hands and was pressing out hamburger patties before I could protest.

He shrugged. "Beats the fuck out of me. I was with King in his studio and we were going over some business shit. The next minute Doe, I mean RAY, calls King on his phone and then he's asking me to watch the kids for a while because he has to go meet her."

"I hope everything is all right," I said.

"He didn't tell me what was going on, but he didn't have that 'life or death' look about him, and trust me I'm pretty familiar with that look," Preppy said. "I'm pretty sure if they're asking me to watch their kids though, it must be a sign of the zombie apocalypse."

"Must be," I giggled, loving the interesting places his mind went.

"Seriously, zombie apocalypse is seriously the only reason I could think of why they would want me to look after their little sex trophies when they've got lots of other people to call on."

"First of all, they've seen how great you are with Bo, so that's Bullshit. Second of all, sex trophies?" I asked.

"Yeah, you know, cause they're a product of..."

"Uh, I get it. I know how that works, Preppy."

"Oh DO you?" he asked, wagging an eyebrow.

"Shit," I said, as a realization kicked in. "The grill doesn't work. It's ancient so I put it to the curb with the trash last week. Should we make the burgers in a pan or bake them in the oven?"

"Blasphemy!" Preppy shouted, gasping and looking around like he was making sure no one else heard me. He lowered his voice to a whisper. "You do realize you're in the south, right?"

"Uh, yeah, but what does that mean? That doesn't automatically give us a working grill." I jumped up to sit on the counter, my legs dangling against the cabinet as I watched Preppy move around the kitchen with ease.

"That means that us southern boys can pretty much make a grill out of anything," Preppy said, plating the last burger. "I'm like a redneck MacGyver."

"Oh yeah? Prove it," I said, teasingly.

"What do you want to bet?" Preppy stalked across the kitchen, getting as close as he could to me with only the tray of burgers between us. My body zinged and hummed like a light being turned on for the first time in a long time.

"What do you got? I asked, suggestively.

Bo appeared in the kitchen, rubbing his eyes with the ball of his hand and yawning. "Bo, my man! Just in time. You must come with me so we can do man things!" Preppy said with as deep a voice as he could muster. He beat his closed fists on his chest.

Bo smiled and was instantly awake as he followed Preppy out into the back yard. "Man the mac and cheese, woman! We will be right back," he said, shutting the sliding glass door.

As crazy and silly as that man could be, I wouldn't have it any other way. It took a lot of crazy to put up with me and Samuel Clearwater was my kind of crazy.

I finished up the mac and cheese and put it in the oven to

warm while Preppy took all three kids through the back gate into the open field. They were gone for about twenty minutes when they'd come back carrying a clay pot and an old shopping cart.

"Why do people always dump their garbage next to the tracks?" I asked as Preppy set the cart sideways over the clay pot.

"What garbage?" Preppy asked, taking a step back. "This is a state of the art cooking machine, right kids?" All three kids nodded or cheered enthusiastically as they watched Preppy turn junk into a grill. A half an hour later the four of us sat on the steps in the back yard as the sun set, eating mac and cheese, and burgers cooked on a shopping cart.

The kids finished their food and started a squealing game of tag in which Oscar decided he wanted to be a part of, bumping between kids and practically hopping around as they ran from one side of the yard to the other.

Preppy shifted next to me so that our thighs were touching. He took my hand in his and the warmth of his palm ran up my arm straight into my heart. "You know," he said, caressing my hand with his thumb. "You've done a really, really great job with the place." Preppy pointed through the sliders into the living room of the house. "I know you were talking about getting a job as a counselor, but personally I think this is what you should be doing. Building stuff. Designing stuff. Making old shit look new again. You're amazing at it."

"I've been thinking about it," I admitted, blushing at his compliment. "But it's not as noble as being a drug counselor but I do love it." I chewed on my bottom lip.

"Noble isn't really a thing where I come from," Preppy laughed. "You don't have to have a noble profession, Dre. You just have to be happy. Shit, you don't have to have a profession at all. But if you're really great at all this. And you should do more than furniture. Fuck, do a whole house. When you're done fixing it up do the design of the inside, furniture and all. I'm sure people would snap that up real quick and there's no shortage of houses that need fixin' round town after the real estate market crashed."

"That's a great idea in theory, Preppy. But houses are a lot more expensive than furniture," I pointed out. "And you already managed to buy this one without me knowing."

Preppy tipped my chin up so our eyes met. "You leave that up to me, okay? Let me take care of you," he said with sincerity in his sparkling amber eyes.

I grinned like a schoolgirl. My stomach flipped. "Okay," I whispered, because there was no arguing with Preppy. There never was. Even if his side of the argument bordered on the ridiculous, he would still win.

Every. Single. Time.

Even with a possible threat looming over our heads, I was still thinking how lucky I was up until the gate on the side of the yard squeaked open. Preppy and I stood and walked over to stand in the way of where the kids were sitting in a circle playing with ladybugs in the grass. The three of them were completely unaware of the bloodied man being carried by his shoulders into the yard by two of Bear's bikers. His one eye swollen shut, his cheek split open, his hair coated in sticky red. His clothes tattered and stained. The bikers set him down on his knees on the grass.

Preppy was the first to recognize him. He took a step forward.

"Kevin?"

CHAPTER EIGHT

PREPPY

"**W**HAT THE FUCK happened?" I asked, glancing between Wolf and Rev. "You two?"

Wolf held up his hands defensively. "Not us, brother. The kid came limping up the driveway bleeding and beat to shit. Someone got him good, but it wasn't us."

"I'm fiiiiiine," Kevin moaned, dropping his elbows onto the grass almost like he was fighting the need to lie down.

"Yeah, you look it," I said, rolling my eyes. Stubborn son-of-a-bitch.

Behind me I heard Dre shuffling the kids inside the house.

"You want us to carry him in?" Rev asked, resting his hands on his belt.

"We're good here," I said. "Thanks." The bikers left the yard to go back to their posts at the front of the house.

"Anything broken?" I asked, squatting down next to Kevin.

"Just my spirit, my pride," he groaned. I grabbed him by the elbows and pulled him up into a sitting position. He winced and hissed through his teeth. "And maybe my collarbone."

"Well, there's good news and bad news," I started. "The bad news is that there ain't shit you can do about a broken collarbone. I know, because I broke mine twice and had mine broken twice more." I paused. "Do you want to hear the good news?"

"Suuuuuuure," Kevin sang, looking up at me through his one eye that wasn't swollen shut.

"The good news is that you CAN do something about your broken spirit and pride."

I lit two cigarettes and passed one to Kevin. "Oh yeah? And how exactly do I do that?"

I leaned in close. "You can start by telling me who the fuck did this to you."

Kevin's face reddened with embarrassment as he told me the story of how he'd been robbed by a trio of douchebags over The Causeway he'd met up with thinking they wanted to buy weed. The guys were having a 'boy's weekend.' Apparently, this 'boy's weekend' included jacking my little brother of his stash, his bike, then beating the shit out of him for funsies.

Kevin would be sore as shit for the next few days, but he'd survive.

Too bad I couldn't say the same for the douchebags.

"Can you walk?" I asked.

"Yeah," Kevin groaned as I helped him stand. "I think so."

"Good, then let's go," I said.

"Where are we going?"

"It's time for another lesson," I said. "Except this time you'll be the one teaching it."

"What kind of lesson?"

"The most important one." I was already unbuttoning the cuffs of my sleeves, rolling them up above my elbows. I pulled my gun from my pants and shoved it into Kevin's surprised hands. I clapped him on the shoulder. "You don't fuck with Samuel Clearwater."

WE WERE ON the beach watching the three bitches who jacked Kevin through an opening in the tall grass. It was dark, almost midnight, but the lights from the nearby hotel gave off just enough light to properly see our targets who were gathered around a small fire pit, drinking beers and laughing amongst themselves.

They wouldn't be laughing long.

"What are you going to do?" Kevin asked.

"You'll see. Just stay behind me for now." I took off my shoes and carried them in my hands, strolling by them like I was any other citizen taking a stroll to feel the cool sand between their toes.

I'm not gonna lie, it did feel kind of spectacular.

I'd just about passed them when I spun my head back around. The three of them watched as I approached. "Hey, how you doing, man?" I asked enthusiastically. "It's been so fucking long."

In my head I'd given them names. Dickbag #1, #2, and #3.

Dickbag #1, who was standing with his leg propped up on a log like Captain fucking Morgan, looked over at me and squinted. "Um. Yeah, it has been while, man," he said, confusion all over his face as he tried to place me.

"Come on in here, give your old friend a hug," I said reaching for his hand and pulling him in for a bro hug. Except when he made a move to step back I reached for my gun and before he knew what was happening I pistol-whipped him across the side of the face, knocking him out cold. I covered my mouth with my hand. "Oops, I guess we didn't know each other after all."

"What the fuck?" Dickbag #2 said, standing up from his chair.

"You sit the fuck back down," I ordered, training my gun on him. "Kevin, come on out here," I called. Kevin stepped out of the shadows.

Dickbag #2 swore. "Fuck."

"You guys have already met my brother, Kevin, right?" I asked, pointing my gun from one shivering dickbag to the other. "You guys must be from out of town," I said.

Dickbag #3 shook his head. "No, we're from Coral Pines."

"Then you should fucking know better than to mess with me and mine," I said.

"Who...who are you?" Dickbag #3 asked.

"Oh, shit, my bad. I didn't introduce myself yet." I cleared my throat. "Let's start over. My name is Samuel Clearwater."

"Oh shit!" Dickbag #2 yelled. He tried to make a run for it but before he could leap over the log he was sitting on I fired, landing a shot in the back of his thigh. He crumbled to the sand and pressed his hand over the wound, wailing like I'd just killed his mama. I rolled my eyes. "Shut the fuck up. I've been shot like," I paused to count on my fingers. "Well, at least like three times and it doesn't hurt that fucking bad. Don't be a pussy. Take your punishment like a man."

I turned to the Dickbag #3 "Tell him that being shot doesn't hurt that bad."

"I've never been..." he started. I fired one off, pegging him in the foot.

"Kevin, get your shit back," I said.

Kevin opened the cooler and pulled out a bag of weed and a stack of cash. "Got it."

"Now when this one wakes up, you two will need to tell him exactly how it feels," I kicked Dickbag #1, rolling him over onto his back with my foot. "Ah, fuck it, I fired off a round into his arm. "He'll find out when he comes to."

I turned to Kevin. "Shit man, I can't believe I've taken all the fun from your first revenge shooting for myself. Get your ass over here you knucklehead." Kevin walked over to me and I passed him my gun. "You ever fired a gun before?"

Kevin shook his head.

"Dickbag #2, stand the fuck up," I ordered. When he wouldn't stand I stomped over and lifted him up, propping him back into his chair as he continued to carry on like being shot hurts that fucking bad. "I wonder if your parents know their son has a fucking vagina," I muttered, making my way back over to Kevin.

"Okay, now you want to aim for his shin." I stood behind Kevin and adjusted his hand on the gun. I lifted his arm so he was properly aimed at the target. "Stay exactly where you are," I warned the Dickbag. "If you move even an inch he could easily hit you in the chest or head. That inch could mean the difference between an ouchie he's hurt, and an oopsie, he's dead."

He whimpered like an injured puppy. "Who the fuck is raising you kids these days? Is everyone scared shitless? Ya'll should be fucking embarrassed. I'm going to write a strongly worded letter to our congressman regarding the massive vagina problem our youth is facing."

"What if I miss?"

I shrugged. "Then he's dead. Then the other two gotta go because you know, no witnesses left behind and all."

"No, please. I'm sorry. Wait!" The dickbag cried, but it was too late for begging.

Kevin pulled the trigger.

"I CAN'T BELIEVE YOU fell back in the sand on your ass!" I whispered, not wanting to wake Dre or Bo as I unrolled the hose from the holder on the side of the house.

Kevin's shot had hit sand about four seconds before he did. We'd left the three dickbags alive but not before warning them that next time that wouldn't be the case.

"I told you I never fired a gun before," Kevin muttered.

"That's all right, I think the first time I fired one I did the same thing except I fell into a thick thatch of sand spurs," I said.

"Really?" Kevin asked, sounding hopeful.

"Nope. Not really. I was pretty amazing from the very first second I touched a gun, but that's okay, we're not all born naturals." I twisted the nozzle. "Okay, now strip."

"Uh, Preppy? Why do I have to hose off outside?" Kevin asked, taking off his boots.

"Because Dre spent all weekend re-grouting the tile in that bathroom. Ain't no way I'm going to let you dirty up her new white grout with your blood, so strip down," I said.

"Thanks for today, Prep. I mean it. I…I never had someone do that for me before. It was cool, man."

"I'll bill you later," I joked as Kevin took off the rest of his clothes.

I turned the handle on the house to the left and the pipes hissed to life as water filled the hose. "Okay, let's do this," I said, turning back to Kevin. I was about to spray him clean when I paused with my finger on an entirely different kind of trigger than earlier.

"Holy shit," I muttered, staring at Kevin and his now naked body.

"Dude, what?" Kevin asked, looking down to see where I was staring. "What the fuck are you staring at?"

Kevin had occasionally done something that reminded me of myself, but next to a DNA test, I still had no valid proof he was my brother. Nothing that connected us as family.

Until now.

"Dude, you're creeping me out," Kevin said, reaching for his shorts.

Before he could pull them back on I dropped the hose and bee-lined toward him, wrapping him in a bear hug. "You really are my brother."

"Huh?" Kevin asked, standing as still as a statue.

"Shhhh…just let me love you."

"What exactly is going on out here?" Dre asked from the porch, flipping on the light. I still didn't let go.

"He's my brother. I'm sure of it now," I informed her.

"I have no idea what's going on," Kevin said, wiggling free from my grip.

"Oh yeah?" Dre asked, amusement in her sleepy tone. She yawned and cinched the sash of the sexy little robe she was wearing that showed off those amazing legs of hers. "How are you so sure?"

I stepped back and pointed down to Kevin's massive cock. "Because of that!"

Dre's sweet laughter filled the air. I picked up the hose again and started to spray Kevin down. "Shit man, that's cold!" he shouted, dancing around in the grass. "And are you gonna fill me in on what exactly she's laughing at?"

"That," I informed him, spraying his crotch with water. "Because I just found more proof that we're brothers than the fact that we think we both were shot out of the same cunt." I grinned from ear to ear.

"Okay? And what's that?" Kevin asked. I turned off the hose and Dre tossed him a towel.

I dropped my eyes to the huge slab of man meat between Kevin's legs. "From the waist down we're not just brothers, we're fucking twinsies."

"Uh, what the fuck, Preppy?" Kevin asked, putting his shorts back on.

"Quick," I said. "Tell me something. How do you feel about pancakes?"

Kevin shivered. "Honestly, I'm more of a waffle kind of guy."

Dre gasped.

I shut my eyes tightly, clenching my fists at my side. I cracked my neck and slowly turned to face him. I opened my eyes. "What the fuck did you just say to me, boy? You better start running."

"Wait, what?" Kevin asked, taking a step back and tripping over the sprinkler. He stood up and bolted through the gate. I chased him through the field while Dre looked on and laughed.

"I take it all back! You're not my brother!" I shouted, tackling him to the ground and sitting on his chest.

"What the fuck, Preppy?" Kevin said, squirming under me.

"You and I need to have a serious fucking talk." I leaned down until my nose was almost touching his. "About the abomination that is *waffles*."

CHAPTER NINE
PREPPY

KNOW DRE was probably confused by my note. All it had said was to meet me at the water tower and she was probably wondering why the fuck I asked her to meet me here, but there was no doubt in my mind she'd come.

I smiled as I heard the ladder rattle, shortly after a delicate hand appeared and then Dre pulled herself up and it took me a second to register the fucking walking sex that was my wife.

I'd been rendered dumb. For the first few seconds all I could do was stare. I hadn't even realized my mouth was hanging open until Dre walked up to me and gently touched the bottom of my jaw, shutting it for me.

The first thing that caught my attention were her lips. She'd painted them her signature bright red. Big and glossy. My cock ached and that was before I'd taken in the rest of her.

"What do you…" she started, but I put my hand in the air to stop her.

"Shhhhh, just let me look at you for a minute," I said. I took a step back so I could do just that. She was goddamned perfect. She had a blue bandana tied in a knot at the top like a headband. Her shiny dark hair fell in waves around her shoulders, curled under at the bottom. She wore a tight black skirt that was high wasted with big silver buttons on the front that made her amazing legs look even longer. Her top wasn't so much a top and more like something you wore under a top. It was blue and black, strapless. Tight around her little waist with a blue strip of ribbon laced down the middle, tied together at the top in a silky blue bow like she was a present and I was a kid who just wanted to tear open the wrapping and get to what was underneath. She wore pearls in each ear with a matching strand around her neck and a thick black cuff around her wrist.

"What are you...?" she started to ask, but I interrupted her again by placing a finger over her lips. They parted and she darted out her tongue to lick me. TEASE me.

"I'm not done looking at you yet," I said. Raking my eyes over her shapely calves and then down to her feet, which were bare. She held up the back platform pumps with the bows along the back in her hand.

"I couldn't exactly climb in these but I wanted to wear them since I haven't worn them in a long time," she said when she noticed what I was looking at.

"In a little while, they're going to be all you're wearing," I warned.

Dre's blush deepened from a pink to a scarlet red. She sucked in a breath, which pushed out her chest. The swells of her perfect tits peeked out over the neckline of her top. My mouth watered and my cock twitched.

Dre was everything any man could ever want.

But she was all MINE.

I groaned and took a step back from her, needing the distance to remember my plan. "As much as I want to put my hands and mouth all over you right now," I swallowed hard, barely able to keep my control. "There is something I want to give you first."

"I have something for you too," she said.

"Well, by all means, you first," I said, making a grand sweeping motion with my hand.

She smiled and curtsied. "Why thank you." She looked down to her wrist then back up to me like she was second guessing something. Finally, she took a deep breath and unsnapped the black cuff from her wrist. She held up her arm and my eyes grew so wide I thought they'd fall out of my head.

"Do you like it?" she asked nervously, biting her lip.

"Do I…" I started, my eyes unable to believe what I was seeing. I grabbed her wrist and held it up so I could make sure what I was seeing was real. Dre had gotten a tattoo on the inside of her wrist. And not just ANY tattoo…it was a bow tie. It was feminine, gray and black. VERY Dre. "No, I don't like it," I said with a shake of my head. "I fucking love it."

She smiled and bounced on her heels.

"Ray?" I asked.

"Nope, King did it. Said that he's been staring at your bow ties most of his life so he could do it the most justice without making it look too masculine."

She squealed when I pulled her into me and covered her lips with mine. I didn't think my heart could grow any more but it was swelling in my chest until it felt like it was going to burst. With my tongue tangling with hers, I'd almost forgotten my purpose for the second time when Dre pulled back.

"Your turn," she breathed.

"I don't know if I can top that," I said, scratching my chin. I kissed her on the lips softly. "But I'll sure as shit try."

Dre gasped when she saw the little black box in my hand. She started to cry when I got down on one knee.

★ ★ ★

DRE

I DIDN'T KNOW WHAT to expect when Preppy said he had something for me but I didn't expect him to drop to one knee. "I know we're already legally married, but we both know you never intended to really marry me, but even when I was being a stubborn asshole all those years ago, you've always been mine."

Preppy opened the box and my hand shot up to cover my mouth. It wasn't like anything I'd ever seen. The band was silver or platinum with a large round black diamond in the center and triangular shaped diamonds on each side. "It seems we both have bow-ties for each other today," he said with a laugh.

I couldn't speak. I couldn't even move. I was stunned in place.

"When we first met, your timing was all wrong," Preppy said.

"Why was that?" I asked.

"Because you were trying to jump, but it wasn't time yet. Now, I think it's time for a different kind of leap, one we can make together." He slipped the ring onto my trembling finger. "So what do you say, Doc? You wanna do this right this time? You wanna jump with me?"

Tears streamed down my face. All I could manage was a nod. Preppy stood and lifted me into his arms. My legs went around his waist and he sat down with his back against the tower, me straddling his lap. All the effort I spent getting ready was out the window in about thirty seconds as we tore at each other's hair and clothes. I was screaming his name not long after that. While he thrust inside me he kept kissing the new tattoo on my wrist and then my new ring, smiling like he couldn't believe it was all real until we came together. Clawing at each other's skin like we couldn't get close enough.

Because we couldn't.

"WHY IS IT that you don't need to hurt me when we have sex anymore?" I whimpered. We'd just come down from our orgasms and I was admiring my new ring, holding it up as the moonlight flashed on the diamonds. Preppy was behind me, kissing my bare shoulder his fingers tracing lazy circles over my clit. "Because it's okay if you need to. I get it. I do."

"I know you get it. You're the only one who really does." Preppy gazed deeply into my eyes in a way that only he could. In a way that told me that he could see right through me. "Baby," he groaned. I moaned in response. Maybe because he called me baby. Maybe because he began to stroke me harder. Faster. "Just because I don't need to hurt you to get off, doesn't mean that the pain isn't there."

Pressure began to build deep inside of me. "What…what do you mean?" I said, panting with need.

Preppy placed his other hand behind my neck, pulling me closer. "Dre, when I look at you, when I touch you. I love you so much it fucking HURTS," he said against my neck, the vibration of his words had my nipples standing at firm attention all over again.

"I don't want you to hurt," I said, although I knew exactly what he meant because I felt the same. I had so much love for him it made my chest swell to the point where I thought I might break inside. Preppy looked down between us to where his swollen cock bobbed with his every move. The head thick and purple, throbbing and glistening at the tip, dripping with his own need. "No, Doc, it hurts, but it's the best kind of pain." Preppy's eyes were half-lidded. A devilish smirk played on his lips. "Look, it hurts so bad even my cock is crying."

I returned his smile, looking up at him through my lashes. I licked my lips. Preppy groaned, placing his hands on both sides of my head, running his fingers through my hair. I pushed him to his back and crawled down his body, giving a quick lick to the tip of his cock, which pulsed in response. I watched his expression darken as he watched me kiss and lick my way around his thick shaft. "Fuck," he cursed. "What are you doing to me, woman?"

"If your cock's crying, then I'm licking the tears away," I said, taking the head into my mouth and swirling my tongue around to taste his salty pre-cum. I moaned, the sound shot straight between my legs.

Preppy dug his hands into my hair deeper, pulling, holding me with more force. His abs flexed as I took more and more of him into my mouth, lightly sucking as I circled my lips around the soft skin of his extremely hard shaft.

I pulled back and softly blew on his wet cock. All the muscles in his arms tensed. His hips bucked into the air. His mouth fell open as he gazed down at me with a lust filled expression I know mirrored my own. "Any better?" I asked, wrapping my hand around the base of his shaft.

Preppy shook his head. "No, not better. I think it's fucking worse," he ground out, looking as if he were in pain.

"How so?" I asked, stroking him from root to tip with a slight twist at the top.

Preppy hissed. "Because I want to fuck you again, but now I also don't ever want my cock to be anywhere besides that beautiful mouth ever again. Those fucking red lips. Jesus fucking Christ, Doc. I thought I'd already died, but you're the one killing me."

"You mean like this?" I asked, taking him into my mouth again. Further this time. Preppy had a monster cock and although I used to think he was joking when he said that it was the honest truth. There was no way I'd be able to take all of him but I did the best I could, taking him until the tip of his cock hit the back of my throat. Giving him all I could because I wanted to make him feel as good as he made me feel.

"Holy fucking, shit," Preppy groaned, holding onto the ground for support with one hand, the other still fisted in my hair. The next few sentences that came out of his mouth were incoherent because I began to slide him out and then back again, using my hand on the part of his shaft that my mouth couldn't reach. Over and over again I stroked and sucked him with my tongue, squeezing him with my lips and hollowing out my cheeks so my mouth was wrapped as tightly around him as possible.

I used my other hand to reach around him and squeeze his ass cheek, pulling him in closer, holding him to me. I released him and pulled him back again, letting him know it was okay to move. He nodded, and bit his bottom lip, watching as he began to thrust his hips upward into my mouth then slowly pulling back out, groaning as he repeated the motion.

Over and over again he thrust forward and pulled back. I braced myself with my other hand on his ass and again he held my head with both hands as he fucked my mouth. Harder and harder until tears were flowing down my cheeks. I watched as the cords in his neck strained with his every movement. I felt his ass muscles tense and watched as his entire body tightened and his cock hardened in my mouth before spurts of warmth shot from him, deep into my throat. Preppy threw his head back and in the sexiest most animalistic roar he came and came and came until I thought I couldn't swallow one more drop of his salty release.

He pulled out of me and collapsed onto the floor without pulling his pants back up. He pulled me down with him and wrapped his arms around my back. "I think I just broke a promise to you," he panted, trying to catch his breath. Our chests heaving together in unison.

"What promise?" I asked, confused.

He tucked me in closer, laying a palm over my breast. "The one where I said I wouldn't die again," he chuckled. "'Cause, Doc, I'm pretty sure you just fucking killed me."

I made a move to stand up, still dizzy with lust and unsteady on my feet. Preppy pulled me back down and flipped me onto my back. "I'm not done with you, not even close," he groaned, pushing my legs apart, spreading them wide as he licked his lips and appraised me. His gaze touching every part of my body. My insides clenched and I felt the wetness pump from my pussy, dripping down into my ass crack.

Preppy saw it too. He looked from between my legs to my face. "Fuck me," he said running his hands up my body as he positioned himself over me and thrust inside in one long hard push.

I felt so full. His cock inside me felt warm and my body squeezed him, pulling him into me further. My nipples tightened and my skin felt alive as he pulled out and thrust back in using the same speed he had when his cock was in my mouth. He surprised me when he reached underneath me, lifting my hips so he could thrust even deeper. I cried out and he groaned.

He pulled out, just briefly, to dip two fingers inside me, wetting them. He pushed back inside me at the same time he fingered the tight circle of my back entrance, wetting it before pressing inside. "I want to fuck you here," he groaned.

He pulled out and flipped me over suddenly, slapping my ass with such force my eyes watered but I didn't have time to process the sting of pain because a new kind of pain had begun. The delicious pain of Preppy sliding his cock inside my ass.

The only time I'd ever had anal was when I was with Preppy and Bear at the same time and it was Bear who penetrated my back door. Not Preppy. But I didn't remember much about that part of it. It was like being in a haze. All I remember is Preppy and the hurt in my heart, not the pain of my body or how it felt. Almost as if I was a spectator watching it all happen.

It burned as he penetrated me. There is no other pretty way to put it. But when he pushed past the tight nerves and further into me I was able to relax to the point where I felt nothing but full and a strange zing of pleasure that made my pussy clench.

"Ahhhhh, that's my fucking wife. You like me in your ass don't you?" Preppy asked. He pulled back and I cried out the loss of him but when he pushed back in I saw stars.

We both groaned and I pushed back against him needing to feel more. Preppy took the hint and started to move. Grabbing my hips and digging his fingers into my flesh he pumped furiously like the madman he was. Bringing me higher and higher into some realm of pleasure I'd never experienced before.

"You're mine. Your pussy is mine. This ass is all fucking mine," Preppy chanted as he thrust harder and harder. My eyes began to water, my throat closed up. The balance of pleasure and pain shifting from one to the other with each push and pull. A tightness started inside me and I clenched my teeth, pushing harder and harder back against Preppy, meeting him thrust for thrust until his hands were on my shoulders pulling me against him and grunting.

There was no longer any rhyme or reason to our pace. It was wild and furious and erratic and when he reached between us and inserted a finger into my pussy I screamed out as my orgasm burst from my lower belly, sending sparks of pleasure through my entire body. My sex clenched around emptiness and my ass tightened around Preppy's cock until he was screaming with his own release, pushing deep inside as his warmth flooded me, spilling out around us and dripping down the backs of my thighs.

He pulled out and again we both collapsed. This time my body ached from the extreme bliss rolling through it. I felt both satisfied and energized.

When we were finally able to gather our wits about us, I noticed Preppy looking over at me. "What?" I asked, feeling the blush spread on my cheeks.

"I died," he whispered, rubbing his thumb over my lips.

"I know," I whispered back, turning to face him.

He pointed to his own chest. "But this is just a bag of bones." He pointed to me then flattened his palm over my heart.

"This. This is my life. YOU are my life. You and Bo."

I looked up at him as tears formed in my eyes. I held his face in my hands and lightly kissed his lips. "And you and Bo are mine."

"Why?" he asked. I searched his eyes and there was no sarcasm, no waiting to drop the punch-line on me. It was an honest question.

"Because, Samuel Clearwater. You're everything." I mimicked his own movements by rubbing my thumb against his cheek. "Because you are the light in all of my dark," I said, reciting a line from the letter he'd written me.

Preppy pulled me close, resting his head against mine.

I didn't even realize I was crying until Preppy leaned in and surprised me by licking a tear off my cheek. "What?" he asked, with a wicked smile. "You licked my tears, it's only fair that I lick yours."

I never thought I could love anyone as much as I loved Samuel Clearwater. But as we laughed together, our voices were carried off with the breeze high above Logan's Beach, and we held onto one another like we were never letting go.

We never did.

CHAPTER TEN

PREPPY

W E'D TALKED AND LINGERED on the water tower for hours. The sun was just starting to rise when I helped Dre get dressed and we headed for home.

We weren't even halfway up the porch when Kevin swung open the door looking frazzled.

"What's going on?" I asked, ascending the steps. I squeezed Dre's hand, sensing that whatever news Kevin was about to deliver wasn't going to be good.

"Bo!" Kevin shouted. His eyes bulged from his head. "He's gone!"

★　★　★

KEVIN RAN TO all the neighbors' houses while Dre frantically searched the house again from top to bottom. I ran straight for the woods. When I saw the train coming down the tracks a million scenarios of what could have happened to him ran through my mind. What if he was hurt? What if someone was hurting him? I picked up a rock and chucked it onto the track screaming, "Boooooo!" over and over again at the top of my lungs as the train passed.

I was about to turn back to the house and check the woods

one more time when there was a tug on the back of my shirt. I spun around to find Bo looking up at me with a worried look on his face. "Bo!" I screamed, raising my hands in the air in a mock hallelujah.

Bo cowered and my celebration ended.

I knelt down and pulled his hands away from his face. "I'm never going to hit you, Bo. You don't have to worry about that, okay?"

Bo nodded as I pulled him into me and wrapped him in a hug.

"But you can't run off like this. Never again, okay? Mommy's really, really worried about you and she's going crazy right now. What were you doing out here all by yourself?" I asked.

I pulled back and Bo signed. *Follow me.*

"Where?" I asked.

Follow me. Please.

He didn't wait for an answer, just tugged on my hand and dragged me a few feet into the woods where the brush was so thick I couldn't see more than a foot in front of me. Bo maneuvered through it with ease like he'd done it a thousand times.

He probably has.

Just as I was about to tell him that a hike in the woods probably wasn't the best idea while Dre was probably going ape shit back at the house, Bo pushed back a curtain of branches over a huge tree stump in the ground with a big hole on the side where the wood had rotted out. Bo climbed through and waved for me to follow. I crouched down and crawled on the leaves following him into a five by five space in the trunk. Inside of it was a dirty Dallas Cowboys blanket. Coloring books that were stained and looked as if they'd been retrieved from the trash along with broken crayons.

"This is where you were?" I asked but it wasn't really a question. I was sure that's where Bo had run off to and where he'd probably ran off to for years when he was being abused by his cunt of a mother and the step daddy I wished was still alive so I could put another bullet in him and kill him all over again.

Yes.

I looked around at the little fort he'd created and my heart sank. I tried not to let it show on my face that I was breaking down inside, but when I saw the little pile of weapons stacked along the wall beside his blanket I damn near lost it. Butter knives, one half of a pair of scissors, a small gardening shovel, and a hand axe were stacked neatly. Nobody defended him, so Bo had decided he needed to defend himself.

"Bo," I said, picking up the axe and inspecting it. "This place is a cool fort. Is this where you came when you lived with your old mommy? When you wanted to feel safe?"

Yes.

"You're so super smart for making all this. You're like a super hero and this is your lair. Move over batman," I said. Bo smiled brightly. I cleared my throat. "But, buddy, do you understand that you live with Mommy and me now? You don't need to come here anymore. You certainly don't need this," I said, setting down the axe, which had a surprisingly sharp blade.

Bo stared at me without saying or signing a thing. He hung his head and his shoulders drooped.

"I was just like you when I was a kid. Do you know that when I was your age that I had the same thing? A special place to go when things at home weren't so good?"

Bo perked up.

"I mean, it wasn't as cool as this. Just an abandoned dog house behind our trailer, but I did the same thing as you. I kept things in there I could use to hurt anyone who tried to hurt me because I didn't have anyone to do that for me," I started. "But you know what? You do have people who would protect you no matter what. You have Mommy and you have me. And nobody will ever hurt you. I would NEVER let anyone hurt you. Do you understand that, Bo?"

I saw Bo thinking and remembered how I felt at his age. Alone and abandoned. How I would feel if I suddenly found myself with a family who actually gave a shit and then I realized something. "Are you afraid that Mommy and Daddy will leave you or make you leave?"

Bo reluctantly nodded.

"Well, let me tell you something. This thing here?" I asked, motioning between Bo and me. "It's permanent. Even if you wanted to you can't change it. You're my son. And in our family a son is a permanent thing. Forever and ever you'll be stuck with us. We'll always be here for you. Your place is with us."

I like forever, Bo signed, but he still looked skeptical. How do I convince a six-year-old of my intentions when he'd been fucked over his entire life? And then it hit me.

"Okay, now I want to show you something but you can't tell Mommy, okay?"

Bo squinted like he already didn't think that was a good idea. Smart kid.

I laughed. "No, it's nothing bad, I promise. But I planned on showing her later on tonight as a surprise, but since you're one of the men of the house now I figured I'd show you first. Would that be okay with you?"

Yes. Yes, he signed twice.

"Now did you know that these," I pointed to the tattoos on my arms and hands, "are forever. These drawings will always be on me." I pulled up my shirt and Bo eyed the white bandage covering one of the worst scarred areas on my abs. "They don't wash off so they will never ever go away. They're with me forever."

I peeled back the tape and revealed the new tattoo underneath. Scars, vines, and hearts linked together two names. Bo & Dre. It was King's best work ever.

"Remember how we were writing your name this week? Do you see your name?" I asked.

Bo enthusiastically pointed to his name. I smiled brighter instead of wincing when he jabbed the fresh ink with his little index finger.

"Yep, my man. That's it." I replaced the bandage and lowered my shirt. "And it's there forever. So you're not going anywhere, just like that tattoo isn't going anywhere. You got it?"

Bo's eyes widened when the realization set in. He launched himself at me, wrapping his arms around me tightly. I kissed the top of his head. "Now let's get you home."

Together we crawled out of his hideaway/weapon's storage unit. I brushed the dirt from my pants and grabbed Bo's hand. With his other hand he signed, pressing the tips of his fingers on the corner of his mouth and then again on his temple.

Home.

WHEN I BROUGHT BO back to the house, Dre ran out to meet us. She wasted no time reaching for him, lifting him up she hugged him so tight I was pretty sure she was cutting off his circulation. I almost wanted to laugh when he looked at me wide-eyed over her shoulder but I managed to contain myself. "Don't ever do that again, okay?" she asked, looking him over. "Promise me, Bo. Don't you ever leave without one of us, okay? We love you and if anything ever…" Dre stopped. "Just promise me."

Bo nodded and signed, 'I'm sorry,' to her followed by 'I promise.'

"Where did you go?" Dre asked. That's when he looked to me like he didn't know if he should tell her what he'd been up to. I didn't want him to feel ashamed or embarrassed.

I pulled a bouquet of wild flowers I'd been hiding behind my back and handed them to her. "He went to pick you flowers," I said. "Don't be too hard on him. He wanted it to be a surprise. Right, buddy?"

"Awe, thank you, Bo," Dre said, holding up the bouquet to her nose and inhaling deeply. "They're beautiful, but you have to take someone with you next time," she said. "Now go inside and wash up. I put your step stool next to the sink."

Bo darted in through the sliding glass door as Dre and I looked on. He appeared again, this time through the kitchen window. Standing on the stool he washed his hands as he was told. He waved when he saw us looking, splattering soapy water from his hands onto the window.

"So what was he really doing?" Dre asked, using the flowers to cover her mouth as she spoke.

I waved back at Bo and gave him a thumbs up as he dried his hands.

"Organizing his arsenal."

CHAPTER ELEVEN

DRE

AFTER THE SCARE with Bo, Preppy and I both decided he needed to feel more of a sense of permanence with us.

He was ours, the adoption was legal and binding, but the three of us still had different last names.

That's why, on a sunny Friday morning, I brought Bo to the clerk's office with me and waited for forty minutes. The goal was to leave the building with the same last name.

The Clearwater family was about to become an official party of three.

"THIRTY-FOUR," a gravelly female voice called out. "THIRTY-FOUR."

I stood up and waved my ticket at Bo. "Come on, buddy. It's our turn." I grabbed his hand and led him to the counter.

"I need two name change forms, please," I announced to the bored looking woman behind the glass partition.

"Two?" she asked, looking at me above the rim of her reading glasses.

"Yes," I said. "One for me and one for him." Bo stood on his tiptoes and smiled at her.

"Hey," she said, dryly. She tapped some keys on her keyboard while staring at Bo. "What are the reasons for the name changes? Divorce, marriage, adoption, emancipation…"

"Marriage for me. Adoption for him."

"Do you have your certificate of legal adoption finalization form and your marriage license?" she droned.

I passed her Bo's forms but realized I'd forgotten to bring the marriage license. It was fake, but they didn't have to know that. "Crap, I forgot the marriage license, can you please look it up for me?"

"You're going to have to fill out these forms before I can do that." She passed me a pink and yellow form, the kind that makes a duplicate underneath while you write. "You can use the pencils in the corner over there," she said, pointing to the far wall with an empty table and several chairs. All of which were occupied by people filling out the same kind of forms I now had in my hands. "Or you can fill it out on the computer over there." She pointed to the older model PC on the other side of the room. "When you're done, take another number."

"Oh, but I just…"

"Number THIRTY-FIVE!" she called.

"Come on, Bo," I said, opting for the computer since there was no one there I sat down and propped Bo up on my lap.

The form I needed pulled right up when I clicked NAME CHANGE APPLICATION. It was a relatively simple form but the computer hated me. "See? We can do this, right?" I asked. Bo nodded, but was fixated with a patch of mold growing on the ceiling tile above us.

Current last name was the first field I had to fill out. I entered CAPULET and pressed enter instead of TAB. A new screen pulled up with everything in the county public records that had to do with the last name Capulet popped up, including the transfer of the deed from Mirna's house. "Shit," I swore. Bo looked up at me and flashed me a knowing smile. "I mean shoot. Shoot," I corrected, mussing his hair.

I closed all the tabs I didn't need and went back to the form. I'd only gotten to the second line to fill in my new last name and I'd already hit the enter key again instead of the tab key after typing Clearwater. "GGGGrrrr," I growled at the computer as a dozen or so tabs popped up on the screen again, covering my form.

Bo bared his teeth and folded his hands against his chest like paws. "You make a great little lion," I told him.

I closed out the tabs that were mostly address change forms. People moving from Logan's Beach to Clearwater, Florida.

I was about to close out the last tab when something caught my eye. It wasn't an address change form. It was a lawsuit.

Nancy Clearwater Bateman vs. Mutual Life of Nassau.

Mutual Life of Nassau was a well-known life insurance company with a catchy jingle in their commercials that was hard to forget. I scanned the document quickly and basically came to understand that Nancy was suing Mutual Life for failing to pay on policy number #456479874840, but it didn't give any information on the policy itself. Mutual Life had countered that Nancy had made a late payment on the policy and there was a lot of back and forth statements and paperwork filed between the two parties. I drummed my foot against the desk, knowing in my heart what was coming when I closed the tab, revealing the next document, the resolution of lawsuit.

The one where Mutual Life Insurance of Nassau had agreed to pay one Nancy Clearwater Bateman, beneficiary, a hundred thousand dollars on the life insurance policy taken out in the name of her son.

Samuel Clearwater.

★ ★ ★

PREPPY

DRE HAD BEEN acting strange since she'd gotten home. After Bo went to bed she grabbed a chair that she'd been working on reupholstering and flipped it upside down in the middle of the living room. Kevin and I watched *American Ninja Warrior* as she grunted and swore at the chair, wrestling with a staple that wouldn't come loose. "You want my help?" I asked.

Dre didn't answer and I wasn't sure if she hadn't heard me or if she was ignoring me. Finally, she threw down her pliers and stormed off into our room.

"What do I do?" I asked Kevin.

"I don't know," he said, taking a sip of his beer. "But you better fix it 'cause chances are, it's probably all your fault."

"True story, man." I got up and was about to go find Dre and fix whatever was bothering her when she appeared with a big purse, one I didn't see her carry that often, slung around her shoulder.

"Hey," she said, when she practically ran into me.

"Hey," I said back. "Where you running off too?"

"Oh, I'm just gonna run to the discount fabric store and get supplies for the chair. I don't have the right staples and the plier is all bent and wonky. Maybe while I'm there I'll check out some new fabric for the couch too. I won't be too long though," she said all in one breath.

"They're still open?" I asked, checking my watch. "It's eight o'clock."

"They're open until ten," she replied.

"It's Sunday," I reminded her.

"Um yeah, I was surprised they're open so late too." She looked over my shoulder. "Kevin can I take your car?"

"Uh huh," he called from the couch, his focus solely on the TV.

"Why don't you take mine?" I asked, offering her my keys. She dangled Kevin's keys, which hung from his dirty rabbit's foot keychain.

"Because I'd like to get there sometime today and if I took yours I'd be driving two miles an hour the entire way, afraid I might do something to hurt it," she said. "I could play bumper cars with Kevin's piece of shit and he'd never even notice."

"Hey," Kevin called out, still not turning around. "It might be true but that doesn't mean it don't hurt any less."

She stood on her tiptoes and planted a kiss on my lips. Nothing about her reasons for leaving, or that kiss, felt right.

Not a damn fucking thing.

"Take Wolf with you," I said.

"Don't be silly. I'll be really quick, no one is looking for me at the fabric store," Dre said, darting out the door.

I stood on the porch and watched her pull out. She was really adorable if she thought she was going somewhere unprotected when a threat could still be out there. We'd eliminated everyone on the list we'd made but since we couldn't be sure we took out the person responsible for trying to get to Dre, it would always be in the back of my mind. Which was why Wolf was still standing guard at the house.

"You want me to follow her?" Wolf asked.

"Nope," I said, watching the taillights disappear around the corner before I pulled out my keys.

"You gonna let her go alone?"

I was halfway to my car when I answered.

"No fucking way."

★ ★ ★

DRE

I DIDN'T KNOW WHAT I'd find when I drove to the address listed on the legal documents. Mostly, because I didn't really know what I was looking for.

Never in a million years did I expect what was waiting for me there.

NEVER.

When the front door shut behind me I walked down the driveway back to Kevin's car in a daze. I shifted my now much heavier purse and fiddled with my keys only to drop them when a voice out of nowhere scared the shit out of me.

"You're a terrible fucking liar, Doc," Preppy said, his voice laced with anger and something else that made me cringe and my stomach drop.

Hurt.

"I'm sorry but I wanted to check it…"

"Whose house is that?" Preppy asked, uncrossing his arms and standing up straight.

"It's…I came here to see your mom."

"My mom?" Preppy asked, taking a step back then looking

up at the house. "Why the fuck would you want to come see my mom, and more importantly why the fuck would you lie to me about it?"

"I'm so sorry. I just didn't want to get you upset if there was nothing to be upset about. I wanted to check things out for myself first."

"What the fuck are you talking about?" Preppy asked, looking as confused as I felt.

I pulled the legal documents from my purse, the ones I'd printed off from the county, and handed them to Preppy who scanned them over. "What the fuck," he whispered.

"She took out life insurance policies on you and on Kevin. She's also been collecting disability and social security off both you since you were practically infants. Scamming the system left and right," I started, bouncing from foot to foot. "I think...Preppy I'm pretty she was the one after me or who hired someone to come after me in order to get to you. I mean, the woman collected a hundred grand based on the fact that you were dead and I think she wanted you to stay that way before she either got arrested or they wanted their money back or both. It was just a matter of time. So she used me to get to you."

Preppy lowered the pages and looked at me. "That doesn't answer why you came here to see her. Why you DIDN'T come to me first."

I took a deep breath. "I knew if you got to her first I wouldn't exactly have the chance to talk to her and I wanted to look in the eyes of the woman who denied love to the most amazing human being I've ever known, mother to mother. I wanted to see her so I could better understand your pain. Better understand you before I told you all this and you got to her first."

"Did you find what you were looking for?" Preppy asked.

"No. Not exactly."

"What? She wasn't home?" he asked.

"I wouldn't say that," I said, pulling out the box Nancy's husband had given me from my purse.

"What's in that?" he asked.

"Your mom's remains."

CHAPTER TWELVE

PREPPY

T HE SUN BEAT its afternoon rays down on the top of my head as I stood in our driveway holding a small square of cardboard in my hands. I turned it over, examining every side. The box was no bigger than a toaster. Inside of it was all that was left of the woman who, by DNA only, was my mother.

I thought of a lot of different words when I thought about her and 'mother' in any form was not one of them. Cunt was usually the first word that crossed my mind.

"You sure you don't want me to come?" Dre asked. She bit her plump lip. Awe, she was nervous for me.

I shook my head. "Nah, I'll be quick about this shit and I'll be back before Bo gets home from school. Besides, the bitch doesn't need even more people wasting their time on her than we already are."

She smiled, but it didn't reach her eyes. Like she didn't know if she could believe me. I didn't know what else I could do to convince her that I really was fine. That this was more of a disposal than anything else. My gaze shifted from Dre's when I caught her staring over my shoulder. I turned to see my younger, and not nearly as handsome, brother stepping out of the house, a navy backpack slung over one shoulder.

"What's up, Kev-ster?" I asked, pinching his shoulder.

Kevin smiled and tugged away. "Stop calling me that, man," he ground out.

"Okay, I'll work on another one, but Kev-ster is for sure nickname plan B."

"She in there?" Kevin asked, pointing down to the box.

"That's what they tell me," I answered.

Kevin squinted as if he were trying to see what was inside without opening the lid. "Seems kinda small."

"You boys behave yourselves," Dre said, turning to go back in the house.

"Wait," I said, pulling her back. I kissed her on the lips and she deepened the kiss, pulling me close until Kevin cleared his throat and she pulled away, wiping her fuckable lips.

"Cock-blocker," I mumbled. Dre giggled.

I caught Kevin staring at her ass as it swayed up the steps and disappeared into the house. I smacked him in the arm. "Ow," he said, rubbing his shoulder. "Sorry, man. It's not my fault. She's got a great ass," he said, his apology not sounding the least bit apologetic.

It's not like I couldn't blame the kid.

Dre's ass really was epic.

When the screen door slammed shut Kevin turned to me. "You ready to do this?" he asked, shielding his eyes from the sun.

I gathered the box under my arm and Kevin followed me to my car. He got in on the passenger side, flinging his backpack into the backseat. I passed him the box to hold on his lap while I drove. "Why exactly do we have the bitch's ashes anyway? Didn't you say she was married to a rich guy?"

"Yeah, Mitch. Apparently he told Dre that he found out she

had a secret account she was hiding from him. He said she admitted that she was saving money so she could leave him."

"You don't think that Mitch…"

"I wouldn't blame him if he did," I answered before Kevin could ask the question. "So what's in the bag?" I asked, turning the engine over. I couldn't help but smile when I heard the sweet vibrations of my car coming to life. Dre had given it to me last night, tired of waiting for a perfect moment when our lives were a thin balance between totally anarchy and mild chaos.

"You'll see." Kevin smirked. "Where we going?"

I threw the car in reverse.

"I've got the perfect place."

I COULD SMELL our destination long before we reached it.

"Dude, this place really is perfect," Kevin said, leaning his head out the open window and beaming from ear to ear like a kid approaching the gates at Disney World as he took in the sight before us.

A rusted sign swayed back and forth from the top of a metal fence.

Logan's Beach City Dump.

I put the car in park. Kevin handed me the box and grabbed his backpack. We headed up some makeshift construction stairs that led to the top of a rusted crane looming like a dirty dinosaur over the piles and piles of compacted garbage. My eyes watered from the putrid smell coming from below. "Let's do this," I said reaching for the box. I tossed off the lid and threw it like a Frisbee. It spun in the air until it settled without so much as a sound into the piles of trash below.

"Wait!" Kevin said, holding up his hand. He set down his backpack and got on his knees. He fished through his bag and pulled out a couple of red dollar-store birthday party hats and two of those cheap kazoos with the plastic thing on the end that unrolled when you blew into it like a frog's tongue. "Here, put it on," he demanded. "It is a celebration after all."

"I like your spirit, kid." I placed the hat on my head and positioned the kazoo between my lips, hanging out of the side of my mouth like a cigar. Kevin pulled out a bottle of cheap whiskey and took a long pull, handing the bottle to me. I did the same, relishing the way the bitter liquid burned my throat on the way down. Kevin then lit a joint and took two long drags, again passing it to me.

We stood there with our party hats on, elastic strings digging into our cheeks and the skin under our chins, overlooking my mother's final resting place. We stood in comfortable silence for a few moments. Passing the joint back and forth until the sun began to set over the trees, painting the sky yellow and orange.

"Should we say something? A few words?" Kevin asked, looking over to me.

"Sure," I said, exhaling the smoke and pinching the cherry of the joint. I stuffed it in my back pocket. "By all means, little bro. Go first."

Kevin cleared his throat and took the box from my hands. "You treated us like worthless trash and now you get to be amongst it forever." We both clapped and blew into our kazoos, the squeaky noises they made was similar to stepping on a doggy toy.

"Poetic," I said with a nod. Kevin handed the box back over to me and I looked down at what was left of my mother. Grey ashes and chunks of what I assume was bone. "I'm sorry," I started.

Kevin glanced over at me like I was about to stroke out. One eyebrow shot up.

"Let me finish," I growled at him. He bowed his head reverently and I did the same. "I'm sorry, that I didn't get the chance to kill you myself. I'm sorry you were so worthless. But I do have to thank you for showing me how NOT to be a parent. Thank you for setting the bar so low I can't help but feel like a winner. By being so worthless you taught me how to value the little things."

Kevin gave me what sounded like a golf clap. "Brilliant."

"It was hard, but somehow I made it through." I reached into the box and pulled out the clear plastic bag holding my mother's remains.

"Should we open it and scatter her all around?" Kevin asked.

I rolled my eyes and unceremoniously tossed the bag into the garbage below. "She doesn't deserve that kind of effort," I said. I was just about to toss the box over as well when something at the bottom caught my eye. A white envelope with SAMUEL written on the outside. I pulled it out. "What the fuck is that?" Kevin asked.

"I was just thinking the same thing," I said. "Only one way to find out, right?" I tore it open and on the inside I found two cashier's checks and a short note.

Samuel,

Here is everything your mother took from you over the years (money wise).

If I could give you back everything else she robbed

you of, I would.

Instead, I've matched this amount and have made a donation to the center for abused women and children in your name to help others so they don't have to suffer as you have.

I thought I could save her.

It turns out some people just aren't worth saving.

As her husband it is my job to set things to right again, so this is what I'm attempting to do.

Do what you see fit with her ashes as I don't want them in my home or in my life.

There is no need to contact me again.

You won't find me.

—Mitch Bateman

PS – Your wife tells me you are now in contact with your brother. Please make sure you pass along what I've enclosed for him, as I have no means by which to contact him.

I passed Kevin the note, which he quickly read and then the check made out to his name in the amount of fifty-five thousand dollars.

"Holy fucking shit," Kevin said, looking from the check to me like he couldn't believe his eyes.

"Yeah, holy fucking shit is right," I said, glancing down at my own check which wasn't for fifty-five thousand dollars. It was for two-hundred fifty-five thousand dollars.

"Whoa," Kevin said, looking over my shoulder. I folded the check and shoved it in my pocket, not liking the feeling of it crinkling as I walked back to the car, the stiff corners of the expensive paper poking me in the thigh.

"Mom's dead AND I'm rich?" Kevin started skipping. "This might be the best fucking day of my life!"

We got in and I started the engine.

"You know something, Preppy?" Kevin asked.

"What?" I asked, pulling onto the main road.

"I kind of like having a brother."

I leaned over and rustled his hair. "You know, Kevin, I kind of do too."

The water tower peeked out from the pine trees in the distance. The second big black cock in clear view. The salty air blew into the car and I inhaled it deeply, holding it inside my lungs as if it were the smoke from a joint. We drove passed the vasectomy billboard and then we came upon my favorite sign of them all, the WELCOME, NOW ENTERING LOGAN'S BEACH sign. I smiled like a preteen who'd just touched his first boob.

"What do we do now?" Kevin asked.

I grabbed him by the shoulder, giving him a hard squeeze.

"Now we celebrate!" I shouted, feeling a weight lift off my chest. "Tell me kimosabe, what are your thoughts on strippers and blow?"

"I think, yes," Kevin answered, his face brightening.

I turned the car to take us to King's house where he and Bear were waiting for us in the tattoo shop for a pseudo bachelor party which meant locking ourselves away from women and children while we get shit faced and talk about all the dumb, yet fun, shit we've done.

"Good. That's what we're going to do then. Strippers and blow." I winked at Kevin and watched his smile fall when I added. "Minus the strippers."

CHAPTER THIRTEEN

PREPPY

THE SECOND WE got to King's house and parked, Ray met us over by the car. "Can I talk to you for a minute?" Ray asked.

"I'll meet you inside," Kevin said, heading into King's shop.

"Anything for you, kid," I said, draping my arm over her shoulder. I guess you could say I was taking advantage since King wasn't out here to growl at me.

"I just wanted to say congratulations," she said, but something about her smile seemed off.

"Thanks," I said as she looked to the ground. "That's it?" I asked. "You came over just to say congratulations?" I prodded, knowing when something was on her mind.

"No, that's not it. It's just that we haven't really had the chance to talk much since, you know. Narnia," she laughed nervously and fidgeted with her fingers. "I just wanted to tell you how much I missed you when you were gone. You were my best guy friend. I know we've all been busy with our own lives, kids and all, but I was kind of hoping, if it's okay with Dre, that we could be best friends again because you're here now, but I still miss you."

I wrapped Ray in a hug and kissed the top of her head. "You

were my first girlfriend, you know. Well, friend that was a girl," I corrected. "I know we haven't had time to sit and talk about things, but I think a lot of that has to do with the fact that I never felt like you needed an explanation for things, well, that and the fact that King wants to murder me every time I look your way. I'm sorry, I didn't mean to ignore you. Ever. Fuck, in my mind we've never stopped being best friends."

"It's me," she said, wiping a tear off her cheek. "It's these damn hormones. Your buddy King went and knocked me up again."

"Slipped one past the goalie did he?" I chuckled. "I thought your tits looked bigger."

She playfully slapped me on the shoulder.

"I tell you what, how about one of these days after the kids are all in school I'll come over and we'll do lunch and have ourselves some girl talk."

"I'd really like that, Prep," Ray said. "But let's make it breakfast. You can cook for me."

"Oh yeah? I think I can manage that. Any special reason for the breakfast request."

She put her hands in her back pockets and took a few steps backward toward the house. She looked at me with glassy eyes, some of the lingering sadness from earlier seemed to have lifted. "Because pancakes."

AFTER A FEW HOURS we left Kevin passed out on the floor of King's tattoo studio and followed through with our amazing idea to row to Motherfucker Island at five a.m., which was fine with me. I'd done enough blow to be awake for at least a month. "I'm glad I'm so high. If I wasn't, I'd probably feel how drunk I am," I slurred.

We were sitting on the shore of MFI. Our pant legs rolled up to our knees, our feet bare. Passing a joint and a bottle of Jack between the three of us. Somehow the conversation switched from thinking of a nickname for Kevin to the night I 'died'.

"All I remember is that when the bullets started flying I just kept thinking about Ray and needing to get to her. Bear, you're like a fucking human wall, and Preppy you're always so fucking quick. I just never thought anything would happen to you guys," King said. "I think about that night a lot. What I could have done differently. How it all went so wrong. I can't wrap my brain around it."

I shrugged and avoided making eye contact with King by fishing out my zippo from the inside pocket of my blazer all the while feeling the intensity of his eyes on me. "I don't think about it much any more. It's not like we can change it. What's the point?"

Bear cocked his head to the side and ignored my philosophy on not lingering on the past. "Come to think of it, you were behind King when it all started to go down, but then you moved in front of him until he barged into that store room where Isaac had Ray."

"None of that shit matters now. Guess I just wasn't as quick as you thought 'cause I obviously didn't get out of the way fast enough," I said, whistling while I lit a cigarette.

Bear and King exchanged a knowing look. "What?" I asked, smoke coming out in puffs as I spoke.

King shook his head. Bear smiled. "Nothing, Preppy," King said, patting me on the back and giving me a short squeeze on my shoulder. I passed King the joint. "Not a damn thing."

"Good," I said, looking out over the water on the lights of the town. The town I loved. The town where I lived with my family. My girl. My son. "Now can we get fucking high or what?"

"You mean higher?" Bear asked. "I'll be awake until next Christmas after tonight."

Bear and King changed the subject and soon we were all laughing about some dumb shit we did as teenagers.

Thank fucking God.

They didn't need to know what really happened that night. I'd never admit it anyway. If the roles had been reversed I knew they would do the same thing for me.

Nobody needed to know I took that bullet for King.

That's just what family does. They protect one another.

At least, that's what THIS family does.

"Anyone want to make a gator run?" I suggested.

"No," King groaned.

"Fuck you," Bear said.

But when their eyes met mine they told me a different answer. Within seconds we were all racing toward the water, splashing through gator-infested waters like the idiots we were.

When we were safe on shore, breathing heavily, I looked over to my friends and we all broke out in a fit of uncontrollable laughter. Bear was still going when King leaned behind him and tugged on my arm to get my attention. "Thanks, Prep."

I didn't know if he meant for taking the bullet for him or for the excellent blow I provided for the evening, but either way I nodded and we went back to the debauchery at hand.

Because that's what family does.

We live for one another.

We die for one another.

"Wanna go again?" Bear asked. The three of us didn't hesitate, racing back into the water, pushing each other over in the process.

We act like complete fucking idiots with one another.

CHAPTER FOURTEEN

DRE

"I T'S GREAT TO SEE you again, Andrea," East said, enthusiastically shaking my hand.

"You can just call me Dre. The only person who calls me Andrea is my dad," I replied.

"I was so glad to hear from you last week. Hopefully we can find you exactly what you're looking for." He smiled warmly, revealing two bright white perfect rows of what I would bet were veneers.

"I'm ready to find out," I responded nervously.

East had come by the house earlier in the week and dropped a list of available homes in the area that were in need of renovation. Of the fifteen or so on the list I'd only asked to see one. The second I saw the picture and read the description something about it spoke to me.

Which was why I found myself standing in the driveway of that house with East, the realtor who'd also assisted with the sale of Mirna's house, about to go inside and check out the possible first project of for my new venture. Preppy had dubbed it Dre's Digs, a complete home renovation and design service focusing on reusing and recycling furniture and fixtures.

"Will your husband be joining us?" East asked as I surveyed

the yard and street.

"I don't think so," I smiled. "Last night his friends threw him a bachelor party so chances are they're either sleeping or still up to no good." I almost laughed out loud as I recalled Preppy's middle of the night phone call to slur 'I love you' into the phone while Bear, King, and Kevin threw stuff at him in the background, eventually taking his phone away.

"His bachelor party? I thought you two were already married. I'm sorry, I've been calling him your husband this entire time," East said, sincerely as if the error were his.

"No. We are married. It's a long story," I answered. "A really long story."

"Ah, well we all have a few of those, don't we," East said.

"Understatement of the year. So, tell me, what are the yearly taxes?" I asked.

East rattled off some numbers from the print out in his hand. I nodded. It added up with what other similarly valued homes in the area were paying.

"Let's go on inside," East said. I followed him to the front door. "As you already know, the house is two stories and about eighteen hundred square feet of living space," he said, rattling off facts from the listing as I followed him up the cracked driveway. "It's very cozy on the inside. It has a lot of potential though, just needs some love."

"So what you're saying is that it's small, shitty, and needs to be overhauled?" I asked, cocking an eyebrow at East.

He laughed and shook his index finger at me. "Ah, you speak realtor." He turned a key into the lock. I took a step back from the door to inspect the front again while he grumbled about not being able to get the door open.

The house looked just like it had in the picture. Moldy yellow siding. Overgrown landscaping. Missing shingles. Broken windows.

Fix me. It called out to me.

So far it was perfect.

"It was built in nineteen twenty-one and back in its glory days was probably owned by a wealthy family and used often as a place to entertain and impress," East said, finally getting the door to open by pushing his shoulder against it. I ducked under a spider web and followed him into the main living area. "The Ford/Edison estates aren't too far from here so chances are whoever built this place originally hosted them here."

"Unfortunately, she isn't doing much impressing anymore," I said, trying not to show on the outside what I was feeling on the inside because if I did I'd be jumping up and down saying 'I'LL TAKE IT YESSSS!!!' She might not ever be a place for the rich to entertain, but I knew I could make her not just beautiful again, but functional, and even affordable for the right family if I paid extra attention to my costs and did most of the work myself.

"I have to make sure that the bones are still in good shape," I said "Wrinkles and sags are worthless repairs if they are set on top of broken bones."

"Ah, so you have done this before," East said.

"Nope, that's actually something my grandmother used to say, although I was pretty sure she was talking about something else entirely, I feel like it applies here."

The trim around the doors and baseboards were all original and only needed a good sanding and painting. The flooring consisted of stained shag carpet and torn laminate floor tiles, the kind that stick to the ground like big stickers. However, when I tugged at a corner of the carpet my eyes landed on a beautiful sight. The original hard wood floors. They'd seen better days but to me it was like finding gold at the end of the rainbow.

The electrical wiring was another story. So old and out of code, it ran outside of the crumbling plaster walls, which also needed to be replaced. Also, the plumbing was virtually non-existent. Since the house had been vacant for over seven years, anything of value had been stolen long ago, including its copper piping.

"It's on a full two acres which is rare in this area, most lots are only a quarter of an acre," East informed me as we descended the stairs having just saw the three smaller bedrooms and single bathroom on the second story. The master was on the main level, but would need to be gutted and completely replaced. "There is plenty of room for a nice big deck in the back, even a pool depending on who you plan on marketing to," he added. "Families may not want that, but vacationers or second homes wouldn't buy it unless it had one. Plus, it's the only Victorian style house left in the area that hasn't already been bought and refinished so there is a market for this style home once it's been renovated. I mean these days all the new ones are stucco square boxes that look like they came straight from a house factory. I just came from a new development in Harper's Ridge and let me tell you, they want a million bucks for shine covered shit." East covered his mouth with his hand. "I'm so sorry for my language."

I laughed. "Trust me, no need to apologize."

I ran my hand along the dusty banister, revealing hints of it's original deep cherry finish. I didn't want to just remodel this house. I wanted to bring it to life. It didn't need changing, it needed CPR so it could breathe again.

It was going to be a difficult task, considering all the work that needed to be done, but I was up for it. Excitement surged inside me, but I kept my composure. "I'll need a full inspection report of course. I can't see the roof so I'll need a professional to assess that for me so my offer will be contingent on it not needing to be completely replaced down to the trusses, amongst other things." East took notes on his smartphone as I spoke.

"Of course," he said, nodding and tapping one last button before shoving his phone back in his pocket. "You are a natural at this."

"That is yet to be determined," I said, "but I guess we'll find out."

"What did you do before you decided to do start renovating and flipping homes?" he asked. We were in the backyard, which was piled with garbage carelessly tossed over the fence throughout the years.

"I was in school," I said, almost tripping over a rusted bicycle with no wheels. "Before that I spent a whole lot of time making mistakes."

"Well, Jesus forgives our sins, it's us sinners that usually have a hard time forgetting," East said. I wasn't surprised that he was a man of faith. The 'What Would Jesus Do?' sticker on his bumper and the 'Christ is my Superstar' rubber bracelet he wore were kind of giveaways.

I pushed on the back panel of the wooden fence to test its stability when the entire six panels attached to it all fell to the ground. It failed.

"I grew up in the church. Lost my way for a while, but eventually found my way back. If you and your husband ever want to come by and check it out I could sponsor a visit for you. Ministries of Christ, over on Bayshore Drive," East said kindly.

"Thanks so much. It's not really for us, but I do appreciate the offer," I said.

"Never hurts to ask, right?" East pointed to the plastic piping sticking up in the corner of the yard. "Did you notice that the well and well equipment is fairly new? It was probably put it in right before the last occupants left."

It took a while to go through my checklist of things I needed to see before I made any decisions. I was standing in the living room looking at the cracked front window when Preppy came through the front door, a joint dangling from his lips, one side of his shirt untucked. He smirked when he saw me.

Looking hella sexy.

"There you are," he said, pulling me in for a quick kiss then keeping me tucked tightly to his side.

"I thought you were with the guys," I said, although I was happy to see him. I couldn't wait to show him the house.

"I was, but this is a big deal. I wanted to be here," Preppy answered, giving me another sweet kiss. He smelled like cigarettes and whiskey. His words were slightly slurred and his eyes slightly glassed over.

"How did you know where to find me? I never gave you the address?" I asked.

"You should know by now that I have my ways, Doc. I'll always find you. Always."

"You drove?" I asked, while swooning.

"I walked," Preppy said. "You know, you'd think walking two miles in the blazing sun would make the shit just sweat right out of your system. Well, it turns out that's not fucking true. Fuck, I'm higher now than I was before." He glanced over to East. "Hey, does that guy look purple to you?"

"Nice to see you again," East said, extending his hand to Preppy, his eyes darting down to the joint at his lips.

Preppy held it out, offering it to East. "You want?"

"No, thank you," East declined. "I don't imbibe in narcotics."

"Oh, it's not narcotics, it's just weed," Preppy replied, holding the joint out further. "Although if you want narcotics, last night I had a table full of…"

East held up his hand. "Still, no, but thank you."

"So what do you think, Doc?" Preppy asked, looking around the house. "Think you can work your magic on this one?"

"Yeah. I really think I can," I said, excitedly. I turned to East. "Before I forget, the contract would also have to be contingent on me being able to obtain financing. I'll schedule an appointment at the bank this…"

"No, it wouldn't," Preppy said. I hadn't realized he wasn't standing next to me until he came sliding down the banister, landing on his butt in front of me on the ground. "You won't need any financing. It's covered."

"Preppy, it'll be over a hundred thousand dollars," I whispered out of the side of my mouth thinking maybe he read the price wrong or the effects of last night somehow has him thinking he sleeps on a bed of hundred dollar bills.

He pulled himself up and took a drag of his joint. He looked down at me and placed his hands on my arms. "I know how much it is, and I can't wait to see what you do with the place."

"How high are you?" I asked, turning my head to the side.

He chuckled and scratched the back of his neck. "On a scale of one to ten? I'm sure I'm somewhere around a forty." He turned to East. "Not from weed though, mostly blow. I just lit this walking up the driveway," Preppy explained, turning back to me. "But not high enough to say shit I don't mean. You got this, Doc. I know you do. And I've got you covered."

Swoon.

I turned back to East. "Offer the sellers twenty under asking. We'll put ten in escrow. Let's see what they counter with. Once we reach an agreeable price, I'll have an inspector over to verify the structure. As long as a quick title search can be done we can close in two weeks."

East tapped on his phone again, happily nodding while writing down my requirements. I turned back to Preppy, only to find him staring at me with his mouth open.

"What?" I asked, wondering if I still had cobwebs on my shirt.

"Holy fucking shit, babe. I'm rock fucking hard right now," Preppy said, planting a kiss to my lips. He pulled back. "She's so fucking smart, isn't she?"

"That she is. She's been looking around here like an expert. I almost thought she was lying when she said she'd never done this before," East said. "My assistant is drawing the paperwork up. I'll bring it by tomorrow."

"Thanks, man." Preppy leaned over and picked me up by my waist, throwing me over his shoulder. I shrieked in surprise as he hauled me out the front door toward the car.

"Okay, I'll be in touch," East called out from the front porch.

"Thank you!" I answered, lifting my head off Preppy's

shoulder. He put me down next to the car, opening the driver's side door for me to get in.

I sat and swung my legs in, Preppy closed the door behind me. "Listen caveman, why the carry off?" I asked.

"I had to show him who you belonged to. I saw how he was looking at you," Preppy said, glancing back up at the house where East was struggling to shut the stubborn front door.

"He wasn't looking at me like anything," I said, rolling my eyes.

"Dre, you don't see what I see. Or what anyone with eyes sees. You are sexy as fuck and as your equally sexy as fuck husband, it's my job as the alpha to make sure everyone knows you're mine."

"You could have just peed on me and gotten it over with," I snorted, starting the engine.

Preppy rounded the car and got in the passenger side. "I mean, if you're into that kind of thing, then sure. I'm game if you are. There's very little I'd say no to if you asked. Although, I didn't take you for a golden shower kind of girl, Doc."

I gave him a sideways glance. "You are really high," I said, backing out of the driveway.

"Yes," he agreed, pointing his finger at me. He squinted against the blinding sun coming in through the windshield. "I might also be really, really fucking drunk."

"You gonna tell me how you came to be in possession of over a hundred grand?" I asked, pulling out onto the road.

"I robbed a stagecoach," Preppy joked.

"Haha."

Preppy sighed and pulled out a folded check from his pocket. "Either that or my dead mother's husband decided to make amends for her bullshit by giving me over two hundred and fifty thousand dollars." This time there was no joke to follow. No laughter. He smoothed the check out on the dashboard.

"Wow. How do you feel about that?" I asked.

"I'm not sure just yet," he said, staring at the check. "Figure if it can help you start your business then that's how I'll think of it. I mean, I sure as shit ain't gonna give it back out of some misplaced moral obligation. I've never exactly had a problem taking blood money. But at the moment, I'm still pretty fucked up, so there's that. And for now?" He sighed, folded the check and shoved it back into his pocket. "That's perfectly fine with me."

"Let's get you home," I said pulling out onto the road.

Preppy looked out the window at the sky. "Yeah, Doc. Take me home."

CHAPTER FIFTEEN

DRE

P REPPY HAD INSISTED on taking me out on a date because, as he put it, "We're married with a kid, but we've never really been on a date."

I pointed out that he'd taken me to lunch once at Billy's crab place (pre Narnia) but he simply stated that since I was still unsure of whether or not he was going to kill me at the time, it didn't really count.

That's how we found ourselves sitting on the back deck of Red's Seafood and Steaks, a place the locals loved but usually didn't frequent because it was usually tipping over with seasonal tourists. However, we'd been shown to our table the second we arrived, and although it was busy, it wasn't overly crowded.

And it smelled like HEAVEN. Lightly fried seafood, garlic, and fresh baked bread. I inhaled deeply and groaned. My stomach growled.

"Keep doing that and we're not gonna make it through dinner," Preppy said, gazing at me with a heated expression in his eyes. "And I told you I was taking you on a real date and on a real date they usually have a meal."

"Oh yeah? Where did you learn that?" I asked.

"Google," Preppy answered, flashing me a smile that made

my nipples stand at attention. Seriously, the man was insanely good looking and right there at dinner I officially decided something.

There was no one on the planet sexier than Samuel Clearwater.

NO ONE.

He'd been working out with King like crazy. At first it was just to get his body back in working order after the ordeal with Chop, and then it kind of became a routine he enjoyed. And even though he was beyond attractive before, he was now a woman's walking wet dream. All those new muscles were now teasing me from under his white button-down across the table.

I was embarrassingly wet as I appraised him.

Apparently he was doing the same. "Wow," he said. "If I didn't know you and you walked by me I'd take a mental picture for my spank bank. Fuck that, I'm gonna do it anyway."

I felt the blush rising in my cheeks. "I think you look pretty great yourself."

"It should be illegal to want to fuck you so bad," Preppy murmured, reaching over and brushing the pad of his thumb over my bottom lip. I leaned into his touch.

I gave his thumb a kiss. "And what if it were illegal?" I teased.

"It wouldn't matter." He lowered his voice. "'Cause baby, I was born to break the law."

"Do you need a few more minutes?" The bubbly waitress asked, her blonde ponytail bobbing as she spoke. She'd interrupted us at the very minute I was going to convince Preppy that a proper date didn't necessarily consist of a meal, but can also consist of just animalistic fucking in the location of his choosing.

I was still staring down at my menu but I hadn't read a word. Preppy had been lazily rubbing the tip of his boot on my ankle under the table. He looked completely unaffected while I hadn't gotten through the appetizer list.

Preppy lowered his menu and smiled at me. "I think we need a few more minutes."

"Preppy?" the waitress asked excitedly, pointing her pen at him. "I can't believe it's you. It's been such a long time." She jutted out a hip and pushed out her ample chest. "How you been, darlin'?"

"Been great. Have you met my wife?" Preppy asked, never taking his eyes off mine.

"You're married?" she asked, still smiling, her lips barely moving as if it pained her to keep that expression plastered on her face.

"Sure as shit am. This is the missus, Dre. Dre, this is…" Preppy leaned in to read her nametag. The girl huffed in annoyance. "Tara."

"It's TAR-RUH," she corrected.

"Gdzzuntight," Preppy said. "Can we get two beers while my wife here gives the menu another read through?" Without waiting for a reply he added, "Thanks."

TAH-RUH went to get our drinks and Preppy continued to rub my ankle. "I think I'll get the fried catfish," he said, staring down at his menu.

"Can I ask you something? That girl. Is she someone you…" I let my question trail off.

"Fucked?" Preppy said, loud enough so that the elderly people at the table next to us spun around to see who was flinging around the offending word. I held in a chuckle. "Yeah, probably," he said casually. "Why, Doc? You jealous?" he teased.

I shook my head. "No," I answered, because it was true. Preppy didn't give me a reason to be jealous. His attentions were always on me and I'm not one of those people who could be upset by the past. At least not anymore. "Curious was more like it." I set my unread menu down on the table I leaned forward. "And why probably?"

"Probably is because chances are pretty high that if she knows me and we've hung out that I've fucked her. However, I don't remember her. I don't remember any of them." His eyes met mine. "But you?" He reached across the table and laced his hand with mine. "Not only do I remember every single amazing second with you." He sucked in his bottom lip, darting the tip of his tongue out when he released it, staring at me like he was hungry, but not for food.

For me.

"I can still taste you."

My lips parted and I felt my cheeks grow warm. I was afraid if I stood up off the plastic chair that I'd leave a puddle in my wake. My thighs trembled.

"Have y'all decided yet?" the waitress asked, pulling out a pen and pad from her apron. I still hadn't looked at the menu.

Preppy chuckled, sensing my dilemma. "We'll have two blue crab plates."

"Good choice," she said, taking down our orders and leaving the table.

"Thanks," I said. The sun was setting over the river. Preppy traced lazy circles over my wrists. It was a romantic moment and I felt like I was spoiling it by being so turned on I could scream. I was squirming in my seat like a kid who couldn't sit still. My nipples were painfully hard underneath my blouse. My breasts heavy and full.

Preppy called over the waitress. "We're gonna take a little walk before our food comes." He grabbed my hand and pulled me up from my chair. He tugged me along behind him as we walked down the peer to the small beach below.

"Where are we going?" I asked, trying to keep up.

"I gotta take care of a situation," he replied. The restaurant was half on land, half on pilings, creating a shadowy overhang onto the beach that was already in the dark and the sun hadn't even fully set.

"What kind of situation?" I asked, breathing heavily as he pulled me into the back corner of the overhang. Sand fell as patrons and staff walked around on the deck above us.

"I can smell you, baby. I know what has you wiggling around. I aim to fix it for you by giving you this big cock. Right fucking now." He grabbed my wrist and set my palm on the front of the huge bulge of his pants. I gasped. He wasn't joking. He was rock hard and straining against the fabric.

He crushed his lips to mine and made quick work of pushing my skirt up my thighs. I reached for his pants, unbuckled his belt and his fly, releasing his massive erection. It hung heavy and hot in my hand. He groaned when I touched him, but pushed me away, spinning me around. "Hands on the wall," he ordered.

I placed my hands on the wall as I was told. Preppy had already pushed the strip of fabric covering my pussy aside and was pushing his hard heat into me. I groaned and sucked in a breath when I realized that the people above us could probably hear me. I arched back against him, needing more and more and he gave it to me. Glorious inch by inch until I couldn't take him any further.

"Hold the fuck on, Doc," he whispered the delicious warning in my ear, his cool breath tickling my skin.

Chills ran down my spine. I bit back a scream as he began to furiously pound into me, his massive cock rubbing against every nerve inside me with each torturous stroke. In and out. In. Out. His fingers dug into my ass cheeks while he gave me exactly what I'd needed. What I'd been craving.

Him.

All of him.

"I won't ever get enough of this beautiful fucking pussy," Preppy groaned. "Holy fucking shit." His pace became fast and reckless, a sure sign that he was about to come. He pushed into me as hard and as deep as he could and I thought right then I was going to tip over the edge until he twisted his hips and I lost my fucking mind. I cried out as the orgasm that had started out mild exploded into something not of this universe. I didn't just feel it in my pussy, I felt it in my nipples, in my skin, in my fingertips. Bursts of pleasure that weren't like a wave, but like lights growing brighter and brighter until the glass bulbs shattered all around us. We were still breathing heavily through our recoveries when reality came back into focus and I realized that's exactly what he'd done to me.

He'd shattered me.

Thoroughly. Beautifully. Crazily.

I never wanted to be put back together.

PREPPY

I WANT TO SAY that every time with Dre was like the first time, but it wasn't. It was BETTER.

The anticipation. The need. It only grew, thickening between us with each tick of the clock.

I'd never get enough of her smell. Her taste. Her touch. HER.

Not now.

Not *ever*.

I tucked myself back in my pants and tried to put Dre back together best I could. It was downright adorable when she stumbled around like I'd just fed her half a bottle of tequila, but the truth was my legs were feeling a little shaky too. I held tightly onto her arm to guide her back up to the deck. She looked up at me with the goofiest smile on her face. When we made it back to our seats. I let Dre sit first and pushed her chair in.

"Thank you. So chivalrous," Dre pointed out, crossing her legs and setting her napkin back on her lap. She was practically glowing, and I'm not a huge fan of a pussy word like GLOWING, but there was no other way to describe her.

I sat down and grabbed my beer. "I mean, if a quick hard fuck in a public place doesn't make me chivalrous than I don't know what does."

Dre laughed just as TAR-RAH brought us our food. She cleared her throat. "For the record, I heard you," she said setting our plates in front of us.

Instead of being embarrassed or looking to me to make things better like most chicks would, my wife winked at the waitress. "I was kind of hoping you would." She set the check down on the table and left but she could have been naked skipping through the place and I wouldn't have noticed. I was too busy staring at the swollen lipped little vixen that was my wife as she took a sip of her beer. "Holy shit, I'm getting hard again," I said.

Dre covered her mouth to prevent spitting her beer onto the table. She laughed as she wiped the dribble on her chin with a napkin. "The things you say," she said, a blush creeping up her cheeks.

"Does it bother you?" I asked. "The way I talk. The things I say."

She shook her head. "No. I think the way your mind works is incredible. Hilarious at times, but still incredible. It's unexpected." She pressed her lips together and toyed with the edge of the label of her beer. "You're just you, and there's no one else like you."

I coughed and glowered at the bottle in my hand as if it was the beer's fault, and not my emotions, I was choking on. "I think the way you look. The things you do. The way you are with Bo. With me. God fucking damn it, Doc. You're the incredible one."

She inhaled sharply.

"Now eat while you can because I have a surprise for you," I told her.

"Another surprise?" she asked, eagerly picking up her crab-cracker. She stuck her tongue out of the side of her mouth and concentrated on breaking the hard shell of the crab.

I took a sip of my beer and leaned over my plate. Her eyes met mine.

"You've got a lifetime of surprises coming your way, Doc."

CHAPTER SIXTEEN

DRE

MY NEXT SURPRISE turned out to be Ray and Thia who were kind enough to organize a bachelorette for me. They'd both become great friends in recent months.

They took me to a bar called Hansen's where we played pool, drank pitchers of warm beer (everyone except Ray), danced to the music from the live band, and talked about all things wife/woman/mother/life while pretending like we didn't know that Wolf and Rev, who were standing on opposite corners of the room, were sent to keep an eye on us.

After our second pitcher of beer, I excused myself to use the restroom.

I was in a stall doing my business when I heard the door open. A wave of loud music from the band came bursting in then swiftly disappeared as the door was shut again. I didn't think anything of it until I heard the door being locked. Footsteps slowly clacked across the uneven tile. "Ray?" I asked. "Thia?"

No answer.

I really wished the stall was the kind you could see under but no such luck, the door went all the way to the floor.

Fear turned to panic as the footsteps stopped just outside the stall.

I pulled up my panties and pulled down my dress assessing where I could go or what I could use as a weapon, but there was nothing. I was about to just push open the stall hoping to hit whoever was standing behind it and make my escape when a loud knock came at the bathroom door. "Why the fuck is this locked?" A female voice slurred, followed by more knocking. "Open up we gotta pee," another girl shouted.

The footsteps retreated. I heard the door being unlocked followed by both the music and the chatting girls stumbling their way in.

I slowly unlatched the door and when I emerged there were only two girls in the bathroom. One was fixing her lipstick. The other was peeing in the sink with her red panties down around her ankles.

"Was there anyone else just in here?" I asked.

"No, but we thought the door was locked, but I think it was just jammed, we got it open."

"And there was no one else in here?" I asked. "Are you sure?"

Did I imagine the footsteps?

"No one but us and our fine selves," the one girl answered, hopping off the sink and pulling up her panties. "Wait, were you waiting for someone so you could like hook-up in the bathroom?" The other girl asked, flipping her hair over her shoulder. "That's so slutty, I fucking love it."

I left them behind in the bathroom. The only explanation for what I experienced was a left over side effect from when Preppy's mom had someone attempt to kidnap me. Fear in its most basic form running amok.

She's dead. There's nothing to fear. I reminded myself.

Plus, there was a very important day coming up, so of course I was a little on edge.

Logically, there was no way someone could have been in the bathroom, unlocked the door and left, without those two girls not seeing them. By the time I'd made it back to the pool table to join Ray and Thia, I'd convinced myself that it was all a misunderstanding and I'd let my imagination and fear take over.

It was my bachelorette party after all. I was going to make the best of it.

Ray handed me a shot and I took it without asking what was in it. The clear liquid burned my throat on the way down. No sooner than I set the glass down on a nearby table did a pair of masculine hands grabbed me around the waist from behind. I shrieked, but the voice only laughed. He released me and I twirled around to find myself face to face with Brandon!

I shrieked again, this time in delight instead of fear. I jumped into his arms and gave him a hug that bordered on strangling. "Hey, doll face," he said, setting me back on the floor.

"I can't believe you're here!" I said.

"These girls over here called me and told me that it would be a major life travesty if you didn't have your bestest friend in the entire world here for you bachelorette." Ray and Thia paused their game of pool. "So here I am! You have them to thank."

"Thank you so much guys," I said, leaning against Brandon. I'd missed him in recent months. A few phone calls a week wasn't the same as having him nearby all the time.

"Don't thank us," Ray said, lining up her shot.

"Yeah, I don't even know what he's talking about," Thia added with a wink.

"I'm glad they let a boy crash your party, especially since

they just tossed one out," Brandon said with a wink, tossing down his own shot and wincing with one eye shut.

"What? Who?"

"Oh, he means Kevin," Thia said, sinking the corner shot she'd been aiming for. "He showed up just as you went to the bathroom. Tried to crash our party so we gave him the boot. No boys allowed…" she looked to Brandon, "unless that boy likes other boys."

Thia looked to Wolf and Rev who were scanning the crowd. "Or unless you've been hired to be here for security," she amended.

They all clinked their beer bottles together. "Hey, is everything okay?" Brandon asked me with a nudge. I couldn't help the sinking feeling in my stomach.

"Yeah, yeah, everything's fine," I said, because it was. It's not like Kevin would make his presence known to a bunch of potential witnesses and then try to assault me in the bathroom.

Right?

I plastered a smile on my face. The rest of the night was spent laughing, playing pool, dancing, drinking, and singing off key at the top of our lungs. At no point did I think of that incident again because I was having a great time.

It wasn't even lingering in the back of my mind at all. Not even a little bit. Since it couldn't have happened, it didn't need to be thought about.

Not when the bar shut down and we all said our goodbye's. Not when Wolf drove me home. Not when I turned the key in the lock. Not when I pushed open the door. Not when I slowly walked passed Kevin's shut door before checking in on Bo. Not even when I curled in bed next to Preppy and wrapped myself around his big warm sleeping body.

Nope.

Not at all.

Besides, even if I did have any fears or lingering concerns, they'd have to wait. Tomorrow was already booked solid.

Tomorrow, I marry my husband.

CHAPTER SEVENTEEN

PREPPY

"YOU PICKED A creepy-ass place for this shindig, Prep," Bear grumbled. "Was the county morgue all booked up or something?"

"It's not my fault your as unsentimental as you are a bad dresser," I said, flicking my cigarette. "This place is sweet and utter perfection. Don't be pissed at me because Thia made you adult today and wear a shirt."

"Okay, girls, calm it down over there," King said, his arm around Ray's shoulders.

"Ti said you told her I HAD to wear one," Bear spat, pulling on the sleeves of the dress shirt he had put on under his cut.

"You got played, motherfucka!" I sang in a high-pitched voice.

Thia gave Bear a knowing wave from where she stood over by the front gate. "This thing's itchy as fuck, I'm taking it off," he said, pulling off his cut to remove his shirt just as Thia came walking up to us.

"Too fucking late, Beary Boo Boo," I teased.

"Fuck," he groaned, shrugging his cut back in place. "It's a good thing I'm your best man or this thing would be off already."

"I thought I was your best man?" King asked.

I didn't get a chance to tell them that neither of them were my best man because just then Thia passed Bear and came up to me instead. "Can I talk to you for a second?" she asked, her pinkish-red hair, which was usually unruly and sticking out in every direction, had been tamed into a pile of curls pinned to the top of her head.

"Uh, sure," I responded, following her around to a quiet corner. "You know, I don't think we've ever talked more than a handful of times," I pointed out. "And I could use some new ammo against Bear every so often."

"Talking would be nice," Thia said. She reached into the pocket on her dress. "I wanted to give you something," she handed me a folded piece of paper.

"Ti, I'm getting married today. It's a little too late for love notes, don't you think?" I asked, turning the paper over in my hand. Thia giggled and we both glanced over to Bear who was watching us with his arms crossed over his chest and a hard look on his face.

"Do you know how Grace was always hiding things?" Thia asked, rocking from her heels to her toes.

"Yeah," I said. "I remember that anytime she needed cash she'd be digging something up or hunting in the back of the freezer. She'd have things taped to the backs of picture frames and cereal boxes."

"Well, since we've moved into her house I've found a lot of things like that. A twenty-dollar bill here and there. A coupon for free entrance to the swap meet. A ledger to a bank account that no longer exists." Thia pointed to the page I'd begun to unfold. Samuel was written across the top in familiar handwriting. "This was taped to a truss in the attic. I found it while I was cleaning it out. I thought that you might want it today, so you can have a piece of her with you."

I glanced down at Grace's handwriting, running my fingers over her words. "Thanks, Ti," I said, not able to take my appreciation any further with words because I was amazed at what I was holding.

"I'll leave you alone." Thia turned away.

"No, please. Stay," I said.

"I'm not gonna hold you while you cry," Thia teased. "But I'll stay."

"Deal," I said, turning my attention to Grace's words, written in neat cursive.

My Dearest Samuel,

This might just be a crazy letter coming from an even crazier old woman, but I feel in my heart I have to write it anyway. You may never read this, but I can't NOT write it.

In case you didn't already know, you're dead. Or at least that's what I've been told by numerous individuals who all make me want to run them over with Edmond's old truck. So that's what I've believed all these months. That you're gone. I believed it when I held your blood-stained shirt at the hospital. I believed it when we lowered your casket into the ground.

I've mourned you. Every single day I've mourned you, my dear boy.

But something is missing and at first I thought it was a normal feeling of loss. Loss of light that always surrounded you. The color in my life. But it's more than that. A lot more.

Because when I get on my knees at night and pray, I close my eyes and pray I don't feel like you're on the other side like my Edmond.

I haven't brought this up to anyone, and I know it's impossible, but my hope it that this is all either all a nightmare or I am indeed crazy.

If I am crazy then I wish to save sanity for those who want or need it more, because I don't want to live in a world where I don't have hope that you aren't out there somewhere.

Heart beating, warm skin.

I have hope. And because I have hope, I still have you.

It's the little things I miss about you. Like correcting you even though I loved every word that comes out of your smart mouth, even the bad ones. Even when I was scowling at you on the outside, my heart was always smiling on the inside. Because you, Samuel, are a rare one. Someone who is as smart as they are cunning. Ever since the day King brought you to the house, just a skinny wrinkled-shirt boy, I loved you.

I hope she does too.

And my hope is that when you do come back, you go to whoever it is I've seen the flashes of sadness for in your eyes, and you hold onto her and never ever let her go. You're a good person my Samuel, even if you've never thought you were.

Come back to us and share your burdens with your brothers. With your family. Let them be there for you like you've always been there for us. Let HER be there for you.

Whoever she is.

You are hard headed. The most stubborn young man I've ever met in my entire life and that says a lot considering I know Abel and Brantley and I've lived a long life and have met many, many people. None as unique as you. None as flawed as you. None as passionate and wild and enthusiastic about life as you. There is NO substitute for Samuel Clearwater and there never will be.

Life is colorless without you.

I love you, son.

I miss you more than words.

If ANYONE on this planet could avoid death somehow, I know it's you. So come back. Come back to your family. I may not be here when you get back, but I'll be watching you turn the world bright again.

If I'm wrong. If you are there on the other side when I get there, just know that I'll be angrier than you've ever seen me in your life so consider this your only warning to get a head start.

I love you, Samuel.

My son.

Always & Forever
In this life & the next,
Mama Grace

I didn't say a word when I was done reading, I just wrapped Thia in a hug. She was right. Now in a way Grace was with me. I felt more complete now. More at ease with her not being there.

"You're welcome," she said into my chest. Bear was already stomping over to us. I released her and tucked the note into my pocket.

"You know, I never really got to thank you either. For taking Chop out. I feel like a bitch that I didn't get a chance to do it myself or see it go down but I'm glad the fucker's dead, so thank you," I said.

"Eh, it was no biggie," Thia replied. "Had to protect this brute over here."

Bear reached us and draped an arm over Thia's shoulders.

"You can't seriously be jealous of a hug," I said, rolling my eyes at Bear. "I mean, I'm not jealous when you talk to Dre and you've had your dick in her."

Bear grimaced.

Oops.

Thia actually laughed. "I know, Preppy. Bear told me that he and her and you...I mean, it's okay, I know. I've told Dre I know too, so there's nothing weird between us. I really like her by the way."

"You're one cool chick, Ti," I said. I patted my jacket where Grace's note was tucked safely inside. "And besides, it's not like the thing with Bear was a big deal anyway, it was only anal."

"I have to go help Ray," Thia said, still laughing and shaking her head. "I'll leave you two alone to murder one another. After all, we're in the perfect place for it." She dashed off to meet Ray where she was waiting for Dre to arrive.

"You're right, Prep. It was only anal," Bear said and I wondered where he was going with this teasing tone in his voice. "Because when I look back and I picture it all in my mind, I mean I didn't remember much at first, but now I can see every little..."

"Bear," I cut him off. "If you so much as think of that night in your pretty little head, I'll murder you in your sleep," I warned.

Bear smiled and pulled me in for a hug, he slapped my back. "I would expect nothing less, Prep."

"She's here!" Ray shouted.

"But seriously," Bear started as we went back and joined King. "Who is your best man? Kevin?"

Just then Bo came running through the cemetery wearing a matching light grey suit and light blue bow tie. He even had on a pair of brown suspenders and he was sporting a fresh hair cut. When he spotted me he changed direction, running straight to me until he leapt up and I caught him.

I turned back to my friends with my son in my arms. "He is."

When the music started and the sound of "LIFER" by Florida Georgia Line started to play I stood on one side of the empty grave marked with my headstone and waited for Dre to appear. I knew she was about to walk around the wall, but nothing could have prepared me for the moment I saw her.

NOTHING.

She wasn't just beautiful or stunning. She was walking art.

I coughed because suddenly I couldn't fucking breathe.

Dre's lips were usually painted bright red but as she walked down the aisle of gravestones I noticed they were a darker blood red and matched the rose in her hair, which was pinned low and loose to the side of her head at the nape of her neck.

Her ivory dress was strapless and heart shaped over the perfect swell of her tits. Short in the front, just above her knees, flaring out to a long gown in the back that dragged along the ground as she walked. There was lace at the top to give the illusion of sleeves but it was so light and delicate it looked as if it were floating on top of her creamy skin. She carried a bouquet of wildflowers and I chuckled when I saw the stems were tied together with one of my red bowties.

She smiled when our eyes locked and suddenly she wasn't wearing her wedding dress. She was naked, skinny, and bruised like she was on top of the tower the day we met. Her stringy hair blowing around her face. Then it was her wearing Mirna's pin-up style clothes for the first time. Then it was her on the night I proposed, tight black skirt and blue corset top. By the time she stood before me and linked her hands with mine she was wearing her gown again and I was stuck somewhere between so much love it hurts and so aroused it hurts.

"Fuckin' eh, Doc," I groaned, apparently out loud because the crowd around us laughed.

The reverend starting saying some words but I didn't hear a single fucking one because I was firmly focused on Dre. The only thing I heard was my inner caveman chant. Mine. Mine. Mine. Mine.

Mine.

★ ★ ★

DRE

PREPPY WORE A light grey suit with a light blue and yellow bow tie. It was perfectly fitted to his muscles and I couldn't tear my eyes from him as I walked down the aisle. My stomach did flip-flops. I don't remember walking fast or slow as my father guided me toward my husband. I just remember trying to get to him as fast as possible as he appraised me. A stunned yet appreciative look in his eyes that made me tingle all over.

As I made my way to him I thought I was seeing things. His image flashed from the scary version of him I met on the tower that first day, to the emaciated tortured soul with long hair and fresh scars. When I reached him he turned back into my husband in the tux, ready to make promises of forever. "Hey, Doc, what took you so long?"

"Don't you mean what took US so long?" I asked.

When it came time to say our vows, Preppy surprised me by volunteering to go first.

"I was a boy when we met, someone who avoided and ran from everything in his life he didn't want to deal with. In some ways I'm never going to grow up, but you made me want to be more. For you. For Bo. Now I'm a man who knows it's time to stop running away and start running toward and I'm choosing to run to you, Doc. Forever."

There were several sniffles in the crowd but I couldn't look to see who was getting emotional because I couldn't look away from Preppy. He rubbed his thumb over my hand and continued.

"I know this is where I'm supposed to make you promises and I'll get to that part, but first I want to thank you for being here, for putting on that dress and walking down that aisle. For saying yes. To me. To Bo. To us as a family." He took a deep breath. "I hate those vows where they make promises that sound ridiculous so I'm gonna tell you how I know things will go down and the truth is that I'm probably gonna fuck up. A lot. I won't do it on purpose and I'll never do anything to intentionally hurt you, but I'm flawed and I'm gonna fuck it up from time to time. I'm not a religious man, but I promise to never lose faith in you. Please don't ever lose faith in me."

"I won't," I mouthed, feeling my chest hurt with happiness.

"I may not be much, but I'm too selfish to let you go find someone who is good enough for you, although I doubt he exists because you're good. So fucking good. I promise that I'm yours and yours alone. Body and whatever's left of this tattered soul." Preppy reached out and took my hands in his. "Remember a long time ago when I said we were the same? I didn't really know what I meant back then, but I do now. We struggle. We overcome. We're loyal. We love with everything we have and fight with everything and more. I'll fight for you and Bo. Every fucking day with everything I have."

Preppy wiped his eyes and then reached across to catch a tear on the corner of my eye.

"Andrea," the reverend said.

I mentally tossed around the words I'd prepared, but had no idea how to get them out of my mouth. I took a deep breath and then focused on Preppy and his burning amber eyes. At the last second I mentally threw away my prepared words and decided to wing it, keeping it short and to the point. "I love you, Samuel Clearwater. I'll love you forever and I'll show you every single day how you're not only perfect for me, but good enough for me, and I'll try my best to be worthy of you. You not only saved my life, but you gave me a life. I am who I am because of you. I'll love you now and forever. In life and in death, and especially in the in-between."

Preppy sucked in a breath when he realized I'd used a line

from the letter he'd written me. "Not even death do us part," he whispered.

"Not even death do us part," I repeated on a choked sob.

"Awe fuck, Doc," Preppy said reaching around behind me and grabbing the back of my neck. He pulled me close and kissed me deeply. The crowd whistled and hooted us on much to the reverend's dismay who literally had to put his hands between us to separate us.

"Just a minute, we've got to get to the part that makes this thing legit," Preppy said, pulling back and clearing his throat. I leaned over to wipe my lipstick off the side of Preppy's mouth. I was floating on another level of happiness when the reverend introduced us as "Mr. and Mrs. Samuel Clearwater."

We both grabbed Bo's hand and were about to walk back down the aisle when Kevin put two fingers in his mouth and made a loud whistling noise, silencing the crowd who turned their attentions on him. "Wait!" he shouted, stepping in front of us, blocking our exit. I squeezed Preppy's hand tightly and in an instant my happiness turned to panic.

Kevin reached inside his jacket pocket. "This isn't over yet."

I WAS ABOUT to push Bo into the crowd for safety and lunge myself at Kevin when I realized what he pulled out of his jacket wasn't a knife or gun, it was a handkerchief. He used it to wipe the beads of sweat from his forehead. "It's fucking hot out here," he muttered, tucking the scrap of fabric back into his pocket. He glanced down at Bo, giving him a wink. "Are you ready, kid?"

Bo gave him a thumbs up and the crowd parted to give us more room. Kevin brought Bo back to the front of the crowd.

He produced a milk crate for Bo to stand on. "Whenever you're ready," Kevin said, taking a step back. Now Preppy and I were part of the onlookers and we both exchanged a confused look. "What exactly do you have up your sleeve, kiddo?" Preppy asked.

Hold on. Bo signed. Preppy chuckled, keeping my hand tucked under his arm.

Bo looked to Kevin for encouragement. "You got this, buddy," he said before turning to us. "He wanted to say something on your special day. He's been practicing nonstop."

Preppy and I both smiled and Bo took a deep breath. We were both expecting him to start signing his speech, but when he opened his mouth and started to speak, Preppy had to hold me up for support. I didn't even feel us moving but before I could register putting one step in front of the other, Preppy and I were both standing directly in front of Bo.

"Happy wedding day, Mommy and Daddy. I love you."

That was his entire speech, but I felt like he'd said so much with so few words. He'd barely finished when he leapt towards us and we'd wrapped him in a hug. "That was fucking amazing," Preppy said. No one bothered to correct his swearing to Bo because he was right. Amazing by itself wouldn't have done that moment justice.

It was *fucking* amazing.

After squeezing Bo until he squirmed uncomfortably, Preppy stood to address the crowd. "I realized that I almost forgot something. The entire reason why we are here. In this cemetery for our wedding." He pointed down to the headstone. "This isn't mine anymore." That's when I noticed for the first time the brown paper bag covering it. "But there is someone else who I thought should have it." He glanced over at me. "Someone who should be remembered." He pulled off the bag and I gasped. My heart stuck in my throat like I swallowed a boulder.

Preppy had the headstone changed out. It no longer read Samuel Clearwater.

I dropped to my knees and ran my fingers over the engraved letters in the smooth granite.

Baby Clearwater
Beloved Daughter & Sister
We'll see you again,
in the in-between

I don't know how long I sat there, staring at those beautiful letters honoring the daughter Preppy and I never got to meet, but it must have been a while because by the time I looked up, everyone was gone.

Everyone, except Preppy, who was kneeling next to me. "Where's Bo?" I asked.

"Ray and King took him with them to their house to get the reception ready."

"Thank you," I said, allowing him to pull me up to a standing position. I shook the grass from my dress. "Thank you so much."

"Don't thank me. She needed a place and I didn't. Consider it like a sublet type of thing," Preppy said with a smile. "I didn't mean to make you sad."

I shook my head. "It's like a happy kind of sad, if that makes any sense."

"It does," Preppy said. There was no doubt he understood

what I meant, because somehow he always did.

I sniffled. "I do love you, Samuel Clearwater." I wrapped my arms around his neck.

"I love you, *Andrea Clearwater*," he replied, covering my lips with his. When he pulled back, he threaded his fingers through mine, pulling me past the rows of headstones and through the gate that led to the road. Preppy wasn't the only one with the surprises. I couldn't wait to give him mine, but it would have to wait. We had a reception to attend.

We walked out of the front gate of the cemetery officially leaving death behind.

I placed my hand over my belly.

With only new life ahead.

CHAPTER EIGHTEEN

DRE

OUR RECEPTION WAS a casual outdoor party at King and Ray's house. When we arrived Preppy went to go talk to his friends while I darted upstairs to change out of my gown and heels into a white sundress and sandals so I'd be more comfortable walking around in the yard. I'd just finished dressing when the door opened and Kevin appeared. His tie loose around his neck. His jacket long gone. His sleeves rolled up to his elbows. "Hey," I said. "I was just coming down."

"I just wanted to say thanks," Kevin said. His hands were in his pockets and his eyes downcast on the floor. "You didn't know me, but you gave me a home. You gave me…a family. You didn't have to, but you did and I don't understand why. I don't think I would have done the same. You trusted me. Gave me the benefit of the doubt. No one's ever really done that for me before."

I put my hand on Kevin's arm and felt a little guilty for ever thinking he might not have the best of intentions toward me or Preppy. "Having a brother makes Preppy happy. Family makes him happy. I'd never stand in the way of that," I admitted. "Just do me one favor, it's kind of a big one."

"Anything," Kevin said eagerly.

"Don't let him down. He's had enough of that."

Kevin covered my hand with his, determination in his eyes. "I'd never let him down. EVER. You'll see."

"Good, now go downstairs. I'm just going to take the pins out of my hair, they're digging into my scalp," I said, pulling one free from the curls at the nape of my neck.

Kevin left and I made quick work of the pins. A shadow crossed the doorway. "Did you forget something, Kevin?" I asked, pulling the last pin out and running my fingers through my hair to ease my aching scalp. I spun around, caught completely off guard when I found myself staring down the barrel of a gun.

★ ★ ★

PREPPY

I COULDN'T FIND DRE. Thinking she might need help with a zipper or something I ascended the stairs two at a time but when I threw open the door of Max's room I didn't find her there. What I did find was her makeup case scattered around the floor, the dresser turned over on its side, and blood splattered across her white wedding gown which was crumpled in the center of the room.

"Dude, what the fuck is taking you guys so long? You got all night to fuck. I've got a toast all prepared and I'm gonna bring up some shit you haven't even thought of since we were little punks running the streets…" Bear's voice trailed off as he surveyed the room. "Fuck, I'll go get King." He took off down the stairs.

I ran behind him to search the place for Dre, but in my gut I knew she was already gone.

An eerie sense of controlled calm washed over me. There was no time to be angry. No time to be worried.

There was only time for revenge.

The rest I'd worry about when my wife was home safe, and the blood of whoever took her was dripping down my hands.

CHAPTER NINETEEN

DRE

W E ALL HAVE PASTS.
Some good. Some bad.

For the longest time, my problem had been trying to keep the past behind me where it belonged. But when your past was pocked with scars, much like my arms were, it was hard to forget what I'd been through.

What I'd *done.*

But that's the funny thing about pasts. No matter how far you think you are ahead, it's always there, nipping at your heels, clawing its way forward until it is in your face, bearing its teeth and you're unable to ignore it.

As cheesy as it may sound, the thing that finally chased the past back where it belonged, was love.

The notion of romantic love was something I'd always thought belonging to prior and much older generations of people. My parents had it. So did my grandparents. But I believed it was something that had faded with time, each generation less and less capable of the kind of love found in romance novels.

Until Preppy.

Because of him I knew love wasn't a myth because suddenly

my heart felt so full it was going to break. Love wasn't just a notion. Our love was practically tangible. I felt it moving around between us. A zing. A connection tethering us together even when I thought he was dead.

Preppy's love wasn't 'romantic'. It was beautifully painful. It was the storming-the-castle, take-no-prisoners kind of love and I never wanted to escape from it.

From *him*.

I didn't think I had any room left inside my heart but when Bo came along he taught me about an entirely different kind of love. One I thought I was never going to be able to experience.

The kind of love between mother and child.

Just when I thought we were beginning, it was all being taken away.

I was being taken away.

Again.

I'd been blindfolded. A sizzling pain continuously shot from the base of my spine, shocking me every thirty seconds or so. It caused my back muscles to spasm and go ramrod straight as if I'd been poked with a branding iron.

There would be no popping of the emergency latch this time. No escaping. I couldn't feel my legs or arms. Couldn't move.

Couldn't *scream*.

Paralyzed in both fear and body.

Suddenly, I was ripped from the familiar trunk of the car I'd been shoved into by someone reeking of overly musky cologne. My adrenaline spiked and my heart started to beat a thousand miles a minute, sending alarms ringing throughout my body.

Alarms I couldn't answer.

Unable to put up a fight, I was dragged until unceremoniously dropped. My head clanked against the hard floor, yet I still felt nothing.

Nothing but *fear*.

My blindfold fell down to the bridge of my nose. That was the very moment I knew I'd been wrong about finally leaving the past where it belonged because it wasn't behind me at all. It was standing over me, glaring down at me, a sly grin on its cleanly shaven face.

East?

At first I didn't understand. What reason would East have to want to hurt me. But then he cocked his head to the side and his grin turned upward into a full cruel smile. The smile was full of newer whiter teeth but there was no doubt in my mind that I'd seen that smile before.

Up close.

While he was *raping* me.

Recognition came barreling into me as he started to laugh. The same laugh that haunted my sleep night after night. The same laugh that filled the air the first time he ripped through my virginity while Conner held me down.

He ran a finger down my cheek, but I couldn't move. Couldn't get away.

I was right. East, the realtor, had no reason to hurt me.

Eric did.

"And here I was afraid you wouldn't remember me," Eric said, clapping his hands together proudly. "I know I look a lot different now. It's amazing what getting clean, body and soul can do for your appearance."

Shit.

If I didn't see my arms and hands with my own two eyes I wouldn't have known they were still connected to my body because I couldn't feel them. I couldn't feel anything besides the shooting pain in my spine that left me seeing stars.

"I clean up good don't I, Dre?" Eric asked, gesturing to his white button-down shirt and crisp pressed black dress pants. He lowered his voice to a suggestive tone, eyeing me up and down. "Not as good as you clean up, of course. I knew a little meat on your bones would do this ass good," he said, a slapping sound echoed through the room and I was grateful I couldn't feel his hand on my body. "I've been sober now for nearly three years."

My jaw began to tingle. "Wha…why?" I managed to ask with a slur, my tongue hanging heavy and useless in my mouth. Unable to lift my neck, my lips moved against the dirty floor. Drool pooled out of the corner of my mouth.

"Oh good, you can talk again. This would be so dull if I couldn't hear you scream." Eric crouched down in front of me. His expensive gold watch gleamed as he smoothed a fallen strand of hair back over his head into his slicked-back do. "Why, you ask? Because I wasn't done with you."

"Noooo," I said. My toes began to tingle and I hoped with everything I had that it was a sign my body was coming back to life. "What did you give me?" I groaned.

"You like that, huh? I had to make sure you couldn't jump from the car this time, although kudos to you because I thought I'd planned for everything but you jumping from a moving car while tied in the trunk was not on that list. The drugs in your system are my own concoction. A little Ketamine, a little Chloroform. I shot that shit right into your spine too. You really can learn anything from YouTube," Eric said proudly. "It'll wear off in an hour or so, until then, we're gonna have a little fun. Just like old times." He giggled, covering his mouth with his fingers like a schoolgirl caught talking during class.

"You're insane," I said.

Eric ignored me. "I searched for you. I searched and searched until I figured you must've been dead. I thought that right up until I ran into you in that house by the cemetery. You walked right into my life again looking recently sober and very confused. You were looking to score some H. Remember that Dre? Remember how it felt to stick that needle in your arm? That first little prick of your skin before it hit your vein and the world went away?" Eric chuckled and stood, slowly pacing the small room. "Sometimes I lay awake at night just remembering how it felt to be oblivious to this cruel world."

Insane is an understatement.

"The thing is, you weren't alone when I saw you in that house," Eric's tone turned deeper. Darker.

Angrier.

"I saw you in the cemetery…with HIM," Eric seethed, with extra emphasis on the word HIM. "The same guy who killed Conner. That's right, I saw him that night. I watched from the bus station as he carried you out of the motel room. When I snuck in to search for Conner all I found was his lifeless body in the bathroom. And when I saw you again, in that cemetery and realized the two of you were together, I knew you'd played a hand in Connor's death. Who knows, maybe you did it yourself."

"I thought you were dead," I muttered.

I wish you still were.

Eric pointed to himself. "I got high and jumped off a fucking bridge! I thought I was dead too! It was a miracle I survived. When I came to and I was still breathing I knew for certain then that I'd been spared for a reason. A higher power thought I was more useful here on earth. I got sober right after that and decided that part of God's plan was exacting revenge for Conner."

"I…I didn't even think you liked Connor that much," I said, my lips moving with slightly more ease. Conner and Eric were always arguing. About money or drugs or even whose turn it was to rape me.

"No!" he cried, slamming his fist through the wall, plaster fell in crumbles to the floor. He turned back around and stomped back over to me, sending one of his pointed toe dress shoes sailing into my stomach. I heard something crack and I couldn't even fold in on the pain so I just had to lie there and take it. "You don't get it. Connor was…he was more."

"What?" I coughed. "Were you…in love with him?"

"I…" he started, pausing to take a deep breath to recollect himself. "That doesn't matter. Not anymore." Eric stormed over to a table at the far end of the room and picked something up off of it. It was only when he was crouched in front of me again that I could see the object he'd picked up was a black leather bound book. More specifically, a bible.

"You know, he's going to come for me," I said. "Preppy. He's not going to let you get away with this. He's probably almost here already."

"I'm counting on it," Eric answered with a calculating smile, seeming a lot less concerned than a man in his position should be. "You know that I've been fucking with him for years don't you? I even blew up his car. By the time I was ready to try again, hopefully blowing something up with him inside, the news broke that he was dead and I can't tell you how disappointed I was that I wasn't the one to kill him myself, but then another miracle happened and not only was he alive but you had come back. My prayers had been answered."

I tried to wiggle my fingers. I needed to get out of my restraints if I wanted any chance of escaping but they were still too numb.

"You see this?" he asked, holding up the bible. "This is what replaced Conner and my unnatural thoughts toward him. This replaced heroin." He stroked the black leather cover lovingly. "I lost Conner, but I found someone much better." He looked over to me. "I found Jesus."

"So it's not you, it's Jesus who wants you to kill me?" I asked through the pain in my twisting guts. I wanted to keep him talking as long as possible to give Preppy time to find me.

HOW he was going to find me was another story.

I didn't even know where I was.

Eric clucked his tongue and shook his head slowly from side to side. "I'm not going to kill you. Well, not right away. Now that I've found the Lord, I'll need to exorcize your demons from your body first. Free them from your inner workings." He held his arms out to the side and looked up to the ceiling with his eyes closed, breathing in deeply as if he were smelling something other than the mildew and dust permeating the room. He opened his eyes and lowered his gaze. "I'm going to save you, Andrea," he whispered.

"You're gonna save me, with that?" I eyed the bible in his hand.

He slammed it shut, stood and walked back over to the table.

Eric rolled his eyes. "No, stupid girl. Not with the bible." He picked up a knife with a thick black handle, its long serrated blade glinted against the light as he turned to inspect it, running a finger over the sharp edge. His smile fell, straightening into a flat line. He pointed the blade my way.

"With *this*."

★ ★ ★

PREPPY

I TRACKED DRE from the app on my phone, telling Bear where to turn until we found ourselves an hour from Logan's Beach in a town called Estero Springs, driving the van through a gate with a sign that announced we were entering a State Historic site.

"I still can't believe you GPS'd your wife," King said.

"You can tell me what a stupid fucking idea it was after we find her," I barked.

"Fuck, no. I'm gonna tack one in Ray's neck the second we get home. Shit, maybe the kids too."

"I lost signal!" I grunted, tossing my phone to the floor.

"What does that mean?" Kevin asked from behind me.

"It means that it stopped working," I said.

"How?" Kevin asked. "It's a chip in the back of her neck. The only way it would stop working would be if someone cut..."

Bear shot him a look and Kevin's voice trailed off.

"She's got to be around here somewhere," I muttered as we parked behind a neat row of rounded trees. "Stay in the fucking van," I ordered Kevin who was in the backseat. "Call us if you see anything coming or going. We moved deeper into the park.

"The last trace was somewhere right in that direction," I pointed north.

I pulled my gun. The unfamiliar terrain was the only thing stopping me from running full speed into the dark to find my girl.

King, Bear and I made our way quietly through the trees in the dark. There were a dozen or so small buildings around the perimeter of the property. "All of those houses are at least a hundred years old," King said. "What the fuck is this place?"

"It's the Koreshan State Historic Site," Bear answered. "Some quack physician in the 1800's started a cult and this was supposed to be his utopia. All because the motherfucker electrocuted himself one night and had an epiphany that the entire universe existed inside a giant hollow sphere. Wacky shit, huh? Guess most people thought so too, considering this place is now a state park that rents kayaks on weekends and hosts Mother's Day brunch."

"How the fuck do you know all that?" King asked.

"It says it right there," Bear said, shining his light on a stone in the ground with a metal plaque fixed at an angle to the top.

"Did you hear that?" King asked. The leaves on a nearby rustled for a moment then stopped.

"Probably a snake or rodent," Bear said.

"Shhhhhh girls. I think that's where we need to go," I said, pointing to a large two story yellow building beyond the clearing in front of us. I crouched down and used the beam of my flashlight on the ground so we could see any obstacles in our way without shining the light right through the windows and announcing our fucking presence to whoever the cocksucker was who had Dre.

I ground my teeth.

"How do you know that's where she is?" Bear asked. "There's a shit ton of buildings around here. Could be any one of them."

"Because of that," I said, lifting my light to the license plate of the familiar newer model Honda Civic parked along the side of the building. The trunk wide open and empty. The What Would Jesus Do bumper sticker glowing in the dark.

"I know who took her," I growled.

"I called the brothers. They're on the way. We're gonna need more backup than your kid brother…" Bear's voice trailed off in the distance because I was already halfway across the clearing.

I was going to get my wife.

Then I was going to burn East alive.

I'm coming, Doc.

CHAPTER TWENTY

DRE

ALL THE FEELING in my body came back at exactly the wrong time, right as Eric sliced his knife along the skin on the back of my neck where the scar from jumping from the trunk was still red. "AAAAHHHHHHHH!" I screamed as he dug his finger inside the fresh wound. He pulled out something small, blue, and shaped like a pill coated in my fresh blood. He laughed long and loud, before tossing it onto the floor in front of my face, crushing it under his designer shoe. "Looks like your husband tagged you with a tracker. Guess he'll be here sooner than I thought," Eric said, cracking his neck. "We better get started then."

He turned back to his table, wiping the blood from the blade with a rag. While he worked he hummed "Jeremiah Was A Bullfrog." He made his way back over to me with the blade gleaming once again. "This is going to hurt a lot." He held up the knife above his head with both hands on the handle.

"No!" I screamed, trying to scoot back along the floor but I was still restrained and could barely wiggle, never mind move.

"In your name Jesus Christ I release the demons from the body of this sinner. I cast them from the dark out into the light!" He brought down the knife in one swift motion, straight into my shoulder. I felt the blade hit bone before coming out the other side, tacking me to the wood floor. I felt it all over again when he withdrew the blade, wiggling it around in my flesh to release its hold on the floor.

I was about to pass out. My vision blurred from the pain.

"Get the fuck away from her," a very familiar voice commanded. When Preppy came into view radiating anger with his gun trained on Eric I thought it was all a dream or a hallucination.

Preppy stood there seething as his eyes darted between my gushing wound and the man holding the knife. If it was a hallucination, it was a damn good one.

Preppy was a mix of beautiful hatred and lustful revenge. He was already handsome with his burning amber eyes, sandy blonde hair, a strong body full of lean muscles and tattoos that decorated every inch of his tan skin including the sides of his head, but in that room he looked like pure heaven with evil intentions and I couldn't tear my eyes away. But standing there, nostrils flaring, I noticed a new kind of beauty in Preppy. Darker. More sinister.

Preppy's face was twisted in anger. The cords of his neck were strained and tight. His chest puffed out in fury, heaving up and down against the fabric of his tight white tank top, the kind meant to be worn under a shirt. His suspenders were attached to his pants, but they weren't on his shoulders, instead they hung down around each side of his thighs. The muscles of his forearms and biceps flexed under his colorful tattoos as he adjusted his grip on the gun in his hand.

Preppy was pure unadulterated power, crackling and zapping with energy like a wind vane struck by lightning. An electric aura of revenge encircled him as he maintained a focus I'd rarely seen from him unless we were naked. Which made sense, because there was something very sexual about the way he moved forward. The confidence, the rhythm. The way the sweat beaded on his temple before sliding down his face and neck. Erotic, yet frightening.

It was a dance of revenge and Preppy had taken the lead.

Eric cackled when he saw Preppy moving and responded to his move by slowly sliding the blade under my chin, piercing my skin with the tip.

Preppy froze and Eric looked triumphant that he had the upper hand.

That was until Preppy fired and Eric's bicep exploded. He cried out and slumped to the ground.

"Fuck, Doc!" Preppy cried. He ran to me and frantically searched my face. He ran his hands over my body to check for more wounds. He tore off a strip of his shirt and tied it around my shoulder. I managed to tip my chin to tell him I was all right.

His eyes locked onto mine. "Are you sure? I need to hear you say it, Doc."

"I'm sure," I croaked out. "It's not East. It's Eric. Like Eric and Conner, Eric," I said, the words taking everything I had to form.

"Fuck," Preppy growled, glancing to where Eric was groaning on the floor. King and Bear appeared.

"End him," Preppy said, shoving his arms under me and lifting me into his arms.

King and Bear strolled toward Eric, but they didn't make it very far. The room shook, a high-pitched ringing sounded in my ears. The roof on the far side of the room collapsed, trapping

King and Bear behind it.

Or under it.

"Fuck, we have to get you out of here," Preppy shouted, climbing over debris with me in his arms.

"Preppy, wait!" I shouted with everything I had. He turned and his eyes followed to where I was staring at a red faced and angry looking Eric. His hand shaking.

A gun pointed at Preppy.

"You know, I don't even like these things," Eric said, shaking the gun from side to side with his right hand, his left hung straight and lifeless by his side. "But the weapon isn't what's important here. Ending your life is." His lip twitched. "So a gun it is."

Preppy slowly set me down on the rubble with my back against the wall. "If it's me you want. It's me you can have. Just let her go." Preppy stepped in front of me shielding me with his body. He held up his hands in surrender.

His empty hands made me realize he didn't have his gun. He must have dropped it when he picked me up. I searched around, spotting it just out of reach in the rubble.

Eric sneered at Preppy. "There is no OR, I want BOTH of you dead." Without warning Eric shifted his aim to me and fired. That's when everything shifted and became like watching a movie in slow motion. Even the POP POP POP from the gun sounded slurred and drawn out. Preppy leapt sideways, his body almost still in the air as he stretched himself out as long as he could, like an outfielder trying to catch a baseball. Only he wasn't playing some game. He was shielding me.

And it wasn't a baseball he caught.

It was a bullet.

Preppy landed on his side with an 'UMPH'. The fabric of his undershirt grew red with his blood. I crawled over to him, barely noticing Eric approaching.

"We need to get you the fuck out of here," Preppy ground out, sitting up. "No matter what happens you go to Bo. Take care of him."

I was about to argue when he added. "Please, Dre. Just take care of our boy."

Tan pointed-toe dress shoes clicked against the concrete. Eric crouched down in front of us. A look of satisfaction crossed his face when he realized he had us defenseless and cornered.

When another part of the roof collapsed nearby I used that moment of distraction to extend my foot and slide Preppy's gun between my legs.

"I'd really hoped we'd have more time to get reacquainted, Dre. But it appears that Romeo over here is cutting our time short. Well, that and I kind of made the building explode," Eric sang while staring hatred at Preppy. "Why don't you move the fuck over so I can kill this fucking whore first without having to shoot through you...again," he laughed. "Then I can send you to hell where you belong."

Preppy chuckled. "Hell? Bitch, I just got back from there and I don't plan on going back any time soon. So sorry, but you'll be making this trip solo."

"What you don't understand is that it's all too fucking late!" Eric shouted manically, pressing his gun against Preppy's forehead. "This is just the rain. Soon, you'll be drowning in the flood."

"Listen, motherfucker. I love Bon Jovi as much as the next man, but let's focus less on quoting the poignant lyrics of an iconic hair-band, and concentrate more on the fact that I'm about to cut you open, gut you like a fucking mullet, and feed your balls to my pig."

"You can't do shit!" Eric cried out. "I have the power of the Lord on my side and he says that you have to die." Eric cocked the gun.

"I feel like this is really bad timing on your part," Preppy started. "I feel compelled to share a little something with you. A motherfucking life lesson, if you will." Preppy's breathing became labored. "The greatest gift I was ever given, was death. Because only then did I learn what it meant to truly live."

"That's touching," Eric said sarcastically.

I had to get the gun to Preppy. I would have fired it myself, but I had no shot. I didn't want to risk not hitting Eric, or even worse, accidentally hitting Preppy. I finally managed to shuffle the gun between my legs. I pressed it up against Preppy's back. He leaned back against me and Eric followed him over with the gun still at his head. Preppy folded his arms behind his neck, over my legs, like he was getting ready to tan at the beach, grabbing the gun in the process.

"And since my death was such a gift to me, I'm about to pay it forward and give you that same gift to you." Preppy shifted the gun from his back to his front while Eric was too busy focused on his words. "Now say 'thank you'," Preppy demanded, firing a shot off before he knew what happened. It hit him in the forearm, his gun flew across the room. He dropped to his knees.

"Say 'thank you'," Preppy repeated through his gritted teeth, cocking the gun once again and aiming for Eric's chest.

Still nothing.

"Say fucking 'thank you!'" Preppy roared, sitting up on his

knees so the two men were eye to eye, only a few feet apart.

"Th-th-thank you!" Eric cried out in fear.

Preppy squeezed the trigger, hitting Eric in the thigh. A spurt of blood streamed from his leg onto the floor. Eric slumped to the floor.

"You're fucking welcome," Preppy said.

Eric sat back up, producing a smaller gun that must have been strapped to his leg. Preppy fired his gun first but nothing. He tried again and again. It was jammed.

Eric laughed long and loud. My heart was beating so rapidly I feared cardiac arrest at any moment. Preppy, still bleeding from his own gunshot wound on his upper chest, dropped back down to once again shield me from Eric's bullet. "Remember what I said, Doc!" he called out as Eric aimed his gun at Preppy's head.

"No!" I cried, reaching for Preppy but he turned around to face Eric. "Noo!"

I braced myself for the boom of the bullet meant for Preppy, but it never came. Eric stilled, dropping the gun. His mouth opened and blood poured over his lips, spilling onto and off of his chin like a bloody chocolate fountain.

He fell forward onto the ground revealing the hand axe that had been lodged in his head, and the person who put it there.

Bo.

★ ★ ★

PREPPY

LIFE WAS ALL about sacrifice and my son has just made a big one.

A human one.

Not only had he just killed a man, he was standing there twirling his arms around like he was about to ask me to change the channel from Sponge Bob to Mickey Mouse Clubhouse. Sweetly. Innocently. He stepped around Eric's blood pooling at his feet without so much as a second glance. He pointed to Dre who was awake but incoherent. Her eyes open but seeing nothing. *Mommy okay?* he signed.

"She will be. How the fuck did you get here, Bo?"

Hid in van.

Kevin came running in. "I heard something explode. What the fuck happened?" he asked, surveying the scene, huffing like he'd ran all the way to the house.

"No time to explain. Take Bo to the van. NOW!"

Kevin did what he was told, grabbing Bo's hand and dragging him from the house.

The collapsed ceiling-turned-wall shook, revealing a dusty but alive King and Bear standing on the other side. "You look like you guys fell into a bowl of blow."

"I fucking wish," Bear answered. They both looked as relieved to see me alive as I was to see them but there was no time for a family reunion.

I picked up Dre, ignoring the shooting pain in my chest, and followed King and Bear out into the sunlight.

Dre was dazed from all the blood loss. Her skin pale. The circles under her eyes dark. "I have to get her help. Now."

Before it's too late.

King started dialing numbers on his phone.

Dre's eyes rolled back in her head and she began to shake. Then the world began to shake.

We were only a few steps from the house when it exploded

around us with a boom that was both blinding and deafening. Bursts of orange flooded my vision, bits of metal tore open my skin as I was blown forward.

My wife torn from my arms by the blast.

CHAPTER TWENTY-ONE

PREPPY

I HATE THE TERM 'nothing left to lose'.

Because lying there in that hospital room was everything I had to lose. I barely let the hospital staff tend to my gunshot wound and stop the bleeding, it was barely even a wound. It was a sandspur in my sock compared to the chunk of my guts destroyed the last time I'd been shot. But my injury wasn't important. What was important was Dre and that's why as ridiculous as the idea I just had was, I couldn't ignore it. I'd try everything and anything to bring her back. I didn't care if she was getting comfortable wherever she was. I didn't care if they were ushering her through the pearly gates with a bottle of champagne and three-dozen white fucking roses. I didn't care if she was the happiest she'd ever been and if heaven was everything she could ever want. Didn't care. I was a selfish man.

She was mine, and I wasn't letting her go.

Ever.

I closed my eyes and started the deep breathing technique Mirna had taught me years before. I hadn't meditated since getting out of Narnia, but sitting there next to my wife I felt helpless. It was worth a shot.

It was only seconds, or at least that's what I felt like, when I was no longer in the hospital room, holding onto my wife's bloody hand as the machines she was hooked up to beeped and blink with the erratic rise and fall of her chest.

We were now on top of the water tower. She was awake, standing on the edge just like the night I met her. Except this time, she wasn't naked. She was in a hospital gown splattered with red. The IV tube still taped to her wrist. Her eye and lip swollen and bruised. She looked over the edge of the rail. Her black hair blew around her battered face.

"Don't jump," I said, taking a step toward her. I tried to keep my voice as calm as possible, hiding the fear pitting in the depths of my stomach. Dre turned to me and smiled. I gasped when she leapt up to sit on the very top of the thin and rusted railing. My heart leaped into my throat and I step between her legs, wrapping my arms around her waist and resting my head against her tits. Holding her to me. Holding her onto the tower. "Don't leave me," I told her. "Don't leave us. Bo misses you. I miss you." I felt the vibration of her laugh and looked up into her bruised but beautiful face. Her smile was big although her bottom teeth were coated in red.

"Save me, Preppy," she said, her voice an eerie echo that doesn't sound like it's coming from her mouth, but from the air around us. Her lips weren't even moving.

"I did save you," I argue. "At least I tried to save you. It's up to the doctors now." I held her tighter, but it's not tight enough. It never was.

She shook her head and pressed her index finger to my lips, which I kissed on instinct. "No, you still have some saving to do. It's not over yet. Not yet." She touched my face and suddenly I was awash in an image. A doctor leaning over me and I realize it's not me at all. I'm seeing him through Dre's eyes. The doctor laughs when she tries to cough out her words. Questioning what he was doing and why. "Save me," she said to me again, and the image of the doctor is gone. I'm back looking into the dark eyes of the only woman I'd ever loved. The breeze is now a wind. Leaves and pine needles from nearby trees cyclone around us, creating a wall of debris and a noise that sounds like a train clattering against the tracks.

"But…" I started to argue. I was cut off when she leaned back over the rail, pulling me with her. She's falling and I fell right along with her, but I didn't let go. I couldn't. I wouldn't. Right before we reach the ground she shows me the backside of her hand, which has some sort of sticker on it. No, it's a tattoo. A cheesy yellow smiley face. As the wind rips through my hair and the ground grows closer and closer I recognized the tattoo. A flood of memory I didn't know I had rushes forward, playing like a movie in front of my eyes.

The truth won't save us because it's too late.

We crashed into the ground.

MY EYES POPPED open and I inhaled sharply like I'd been drowning and someone had given me CPR. I was back in Dre's hospital room and my eyes immediately landed on the doctor who was leaning over Dre. He had a needle in his hand, fidgeting with her tubes. He looked up at me with a smile that faded the second he saw the recognition in my eyes. "You look familiar," he said, gulping nervously and pushing back on the sleeves of his white coat, revealing the stupid tattoo on his hand that gave away his identity.

I stood from my chair, reluctantly dropping Dre's hand gently back to the bed. "I should look familiar." I looked around the room. "I died here once," I said, not recognizing my own voice that was deep dark and deadly, full of the anger pulling in my veins. Doctor Gonna-Be-Dead-Soon straightened his posture and was shuffling backward toward the door when Bear and King appeared in the doorway. Right away they noticed the look on my face and all it took was a tip of my chin for them to push the doctor back into the room and slam the door shut behind them. He fell to the ground and scurried into the corner like the scared fucking rat he was. "We've been looking for you."

"What's up?" King asked as casually as if he was wondering if I wanted to go grab a bite to eat. He points to the doctor.

I bend down on the floor over the doctor and grab him by the throat. "So you hand me over to the fucking lunatic biker, you try and make it seem like I was dead, you try to kill me, my wife, and you killed my fucking mother?"

The doctor frantically shook his head.

"It's a little too late for denial now," I tell him.

"No, I mean yes. I did that. Everything but kill your mom. Grace. It was the cancer. Not me. I swear!" he shouted. "At first I just did some paperwork for him. Patched him up a while back at his house when he got cut or shot. He paid me cash." The doctor shook his head. "I was losing my house. I didn't want to do all those other things for him. I had no choice!"

"You had to? Why?"

"Because…he had my sister. She was one of their biker whores. Their BBB's." He waved at Bear's leather cut. "I just wanted to take her home. Keep her safe. Chop said if I didn't do what I asked of him he'd kill her and then me."

"That never happened though," Bear said. It wasn't a question.

The doctor shook his head. "No, that bastard killed her and the rest of them before he could keep his promise and give her back to me." He sighed.

"So when I showed back up you figured you had to take me out yourself? Finish the job? Then my wife?" I shook my head and kicked him in the ribs. "You piece of shit coward."

"I didn't know what else to do!" he cried. When he tried to stand up King pushed him back down onto the floor and his head crashed against the wall, knocking him out cold. "Oops," he said.

"She needs help," I said when Dre's monitors started beeping and blinking. "I don't know what he might have done to her." I ran out into the hall and almost crashed into the nurse that gave me Bo's information months before. "I need your help," I told her, pulling her into the room. She took a second to assess the situation but we didn't have a second. "Please."

"He tried to kill her," I said, offering the quickest explanation I could. I opened his coat pocket and pulled out the needle and little glass tube thing. "He might have given this to her," I said to her. She took them from my hands but continued to look down at the doctor on the floor. "Please. What is this?" I asked, snapping her out of her shock.

She looked down and turned over the little glass bottle. She sniffed it and scrunched up her nose. She pushed it back into my hands, ran towards a cabinet in the hall and came back with a pair of gloves and another two bottles with different colored labels than the one she just tossed onto the bed by Dre's feet.

The nurse took the flashlight and peeled open Dre's eyelids, shining it into each pupil. She gave Dre two injections into the port on the back of her hand.

"Nothing good that's for sure. It's that same shit that kills celebrities when they take it to help them sleep and realize it's good for a coma and maybe a little death, but it's not exactly Tylenol fucking PM. We don't even use that shit here. Haven't for years."

"How much is in her system?" King asked.

The nurse shook her head and grabbed Dre's wrist to take her pulse. She gently lowered it back onto the bed and sighed. "I'm not sure. I gave her something that should counteract it, but it depends how much she was given and how long ago. If he's been giving her smaller doses to make it seem less suspicious when her heart stopped then we have a better shot at her recovering, than if he's just injected her full of this shit."

"How long will it take to find out?" Bear asked and thank God he did because for the first time in my entire life I couldn't find the words. Panic. Fear. Physical pain from every nerve in my body. She glanced up at him. "If this works, it should only be a matter of minutes before she wakes up."

We were all silent for five long minutes. My heart died a little more with each tick of the clock on the wall.

And then we waited ten more minutes.

And then I was screaming in Dre's face, slapping her cheeks, demanding she wake up. "You can't fucking die! You can't!" I screamed, pounding my fist against the mattress beside her head. King rounded the bed and pulled me out of the chair, putting his arm around my shoulder. I lowered my voice. My words came out broken, only every other syllable made a sound. "She can't fucking die," I repeated. "There wasn't enough time. We didn't have enough time. She promised me she'd never leave me. She fucking *promised*."

King and Bear tugged me back while the nurse shot me a look. THE look. She glanced at the clock and my eyes followed.

Twenty fucking minutes.

★   ★   ★

DRE

"WAKE UP. WAKE up!" The voice is soft and feminine. Reassuring and loving.

"Grandma?" I ask, although I can't see a thing.

I'm tired. I want to go back to wherever I just was. Dreamless rest. "Wake up! Wake up!" I hear again.

"Grandma it's too early," I groan, trying to roll over on my side but I'm stopped by something invisible. Something tethering my arms in place. "Come back later. It's summer. No school today," I tell her.

"Wake the fuck up!" The voice is now masculine and desperate. "Please, come back to me. Come back to us! Bo needs you. I fucking need you!" I recognize that voice and I realize that I'm not in my room at Grandma's. I'm standing alone in complete darkness with no sign of an exit. Preppy needs me. Bo needs me. I need to go to them. I start to panic. My throat grows tight and my heart beats uncontrollably.

"I don't know where to find you! Where do I go?" I shout back. A light appears as if it's the answer to my question and it's the most beautiful thing I'd ever seen. One side of the room is blanketed in beautiful brightness and the other side is cloaked in the dark. I reach out for it with my hand. I take a step closer. I'm about to touch it when I come to a halt and shake my head, pulling back my hand. "What am I doing?" I whisper. I slowly take a few steps back before turning around and sprinting away to the opposite side.

The light was beautiful, but I chose instead to run blindly into the dark because I knew, without a doubt, that's where Preppy would be.

"THANK FUCK. THERE YOU are," Preppy said softly, looking down at me with concern etched into his forehead and tear stains down his cheeks. He looked tired. One of his suspenders was hanging loose from his shoulder. His bow tie hung open around his collar. His beard, normally well groomed, was unruly and long. He smoothed the hair away from my face. "Took you long enough, Doc."

"I knew I'd find you here," I whispered.

"I knew you'd come back to me."

"What what…happened?" I asked groggily, my throat sore and dry. The second I asked the question I remembered the answer on my own.

Eric.

I gasped and looked to Preppy who flashed me a small smile. Tears welled up in his eyes. He cleared his throat and leaned in close so that his cheek was touching mine. "Okay, I'll tell you." He sighed. "Your injuries are the product of a horrible sex swing accident. The nurse said it was the worst one the hospital has ever seen. Don't you worry your pretty head though. They've successfully retrieved the gerbil. He's a bit shaken up, but they think he's going to pull through."

I laughed, because it was Preppy and impossible not to. However, it didn't last long because sharp pain sliced through my shoulder. I hissed through my teeth. "Don't make me laugh," I choked out.

"That might be impossible. I'm a really, really funny guy," Preppy said, wagging his eyebrows. He took my hand and pressed it against his face. I reached out two of my fingers and stroked the hair free patch of skin from his eye to where his beard starts.

"I know," I said. "You're also really, really mine."

"Don't you fucking forget it." A lone tear spilled from the side of his eye and rolled down his cheek into his beard. He sniffled and wiped his nose with the back of his hand. His other arm in a sling.

"Did you finish it?" I asked. "Is he…"

"Yeah. He's gone."

"Good," I whispered, my eyes growing heavy. "Where's Bo?"

"He's fine. He's playing with Ray and the kids. Didn't want to bring him here until I knew you were going to be okay."

"Good," I said, willing my eyes not to close. I needed to see him more. To know he was okay. To know that the life we were planning together was no longer going to be cut short.

"You can rest now. I'll be here when you wake up, Doc," Preppy said.

I nodded, unable to argue or put up much of a fight. My limbs joining my eyes in feeling weighed down and tired. But before I could close my eyes I spotted something in the corner of the room. King and Bear, along with a nurse in dark scrubs. They were lifting a big grey bag onto a gurney. "One more question," I said, turning back to Preppy who kissed the back of my hand.

"Yeah."

"Who's in the bag?" I asked, pointing with my eyes to the scene in the corner.

"Hmmmmm…J. Edgar Hoover?" Preppy answered, a ridiculous fake smile plastered on his face that exposed both his top and bottom teeth.

"Try again."

He sighed. "How about I promise to tell you all about it later. For now, just know that it's a really bad guy who did really bad things, who is going to a really, really hot place."

"Hell?"

"The incinerator at the morgue," Preppy whispered. He placed his other hand over my cheek gently, stroking my skin with his thumb. "Now rest, Doc."

"Okay," I agreed, drifting off. This time my sleep was anything but dreamless. All night I dreamt of home. Bo. Preppy.

My family.

CHAPTER TWENTY-TWO

PREPPY

I T WAS EIGHT in the morning. Kevin took Bo back home with him under the strict guidelines of keeping an eye on him at all times and instructions to 'keep him away from the kitchen knives or anything sharp'. At least until I had a chance to have a real talk with him about the pros and cons of becoming a real life axe murderer. King and Bear had a body to dispose of. Ray and Thia were with the kids but they both called to tell me they'd be by later on in the day.

I was sitting out in the hallway so Dre's dad could visit with her alone. When he came back out he told me she'd finally fallen asleep and plopped down across the hall from me on the only other chair. The fluorescent light buzzed overhead, making the bags under his eyes look just as bad as mine probably did.

"You gonna tell me, son?" Mr. Capulet asked, leaning forward.

"She didn't tell you what happened?"

"No, I didn't want to discuss that with her, not now while she's still in rough shape, but that's not what I'm asking you either, not now anyway. I don't want you to tell me about tonight or about the last time." He lifted his eyes to mine. "I want you to tell me more about YOU. I think that talk is long overdue, don't you?"

I'd never cared what anyone thought of me, but Dre cared about her father and his opinion, which made me wary of telling him anything because I didn't want his opinion of me to change from tolerant to WTF.

"So? Go on," he prompted.

"Now?"

"She's sleeping. I'm too tired and wired to do the same and from the looks of it you're in the same boat. We got time and there's no time like the present," he said, rubbing his hands together.

I blew out a long breath. "I don't even know what Dre's already told you about me," I started, rubbing my weary eyes.

"She's told me some things, but I have a feeling there's a lot more." He rested his elbows on his knees and pointed at me. "So why don't you tell me? Tell me who you are so I know who it is my daughter's so in love with. Go on, son." It was the first time the use of the word son didn't make me cringe.

"You won't like it," I said flatly.

"Guarantee I won't. But why don't you just tell me anyway," he said, raising his eyebrows.

I glanced at Dre through the glass and checked the steady rhythm of the monitor above her bed before turning back to face her dad and gave him the honesty he wanted, but after I was done I would be pretty sure it would be added to his list of life regrets. "I'm everything you shouldn't want for your daughter. Loud. Rude. Crude. I'm sure this is the part where I'm supposed to confess to you that I've done things I'm not proud of, but that's the thing, I'm pretty fucking proud of everything I've done. The good. The bad. The bloody. The only thing I ever did that I regretted was pushing Dre away and now I'm regretting bringing her back to this town because then maybe she wouldn't be here right now."

"Go on," he said, leaning back and crossing his ankle over his knee. "I'm listening."

I took a deep breath and exhaled slowly and figured the man had a right to know exactly who I was. Figured it was like ripping off a Band-Aid, so I decided that direct and fast was the best way to go about this little getting-to-know-you session. "I'm just me. Samuel Clearwater. I was born in this shit hole town."

"You don't like Logan's Beach?" he asked, sounding confused.

"No! I fucking love this town. Doesn't mean it's not a shit hole," I clarified.

"Continue."

"My favorite word is any variation of FUCK. I like my whiskey with a side of blow and maybe a little weed. I have a running theme song in my head for pretty much every occasion and I like to sing it at the top of my lungs, regardless of who is around or where I am. One of my most favorite things to do in this life is to give my friend Bear shit 'cause the look on his face is fucking priceless. I love all kinds of movies and I cried like a little bitch during the entire two hours of *PS I Love You.* I dig all kinds music. Country. Folk. Pop. Blues. Rap. Everything from Tupac to Taylor Swift. I have an unnatural obsession with making perfect pancakes." I lowered my gaze to the floor and dug deeper. "Before Dre, there were a lot of girls. A lot. I partied hard. Watched a shit ton of porn, the crazier shit the better. Fucked around with anyone willing, and some who weren't. I didn't care about the consequences when I did things to them they never asked for. Sometimes I hurt them pretty bad. Looking back, I think I was just punishing them. Taking my shit out on them I couldn't take out on my mom. I wanted to hurt them because I wanted to hurt her. For running out on me and making me think she was dead when she wasn't. For making me care when I shouldn't of fucking cared. For leaving me with my shit bag stepdad who must have taken a master class in pedophilia because after my mom left…" I looked up to Dre's dad who had an unreadable expression on his face. "He liked to switch between beating me and raping me," I clarified. "Guess it kept shit interesting for him. I don't want sympathy. Never have," I said.

"Good. Because I ain't giving you any," Dre's dad said. When I looked at him again there was a smile pulling at the corner of his mouth. "And?"

"And… and I grow weed in the guest bedrooms of elderly women's houses in exchange for helping them with their mortgage payments. And honestly? Those ladies are some of the coolest chicks I know. Florida just legalized medical marijuana, we might never legalize it recreationally because we're some pretty backward ass folk down here, but I've already purchased the fields and a warehouse for the medical part. Got a doctor ready to back it and the business licensers and cooperation paperwork have already been filed. Should be in production within a few months. Also, I died at one point. Thought I did anyway because I was kept in a hole below the ground by a lunatic who tortured me day in and day out for the sole reason because he could." I looked up at Mr. Capulet. "How am I doing so far?"

"So far I want to shove my foot up your ass, but part of me

wants to give you a hug, and since that's not happening, by all means, continue." He waved me on.

"You sure? Cause this next part…" I grimaced.

"Yeah, I'm sure. Go on," he ordered.

"You remember Conner?"

He nodded. "Of course. He and Andrea went off the rails together after my stepdaughter died."

"You know what happened to him?" I asked.

He shook his head. "Went missing, probably OD'd somewhere. That's what we assumed anyway."

"It's a good assumption. I mean, that's probably what WOULD have happened to him…had I not shot and killed him first."

I felt him freeze. He uncrossed his legs and planted them firmly on the floor.

"You see," I scratched my chin beneath my beard, "Conner stole from me, which is only done if you are really wanting a bullet hole in your body. He was going to die anyway, but the dumb shit decided to give me more reasons to take him out when I found him in a dirty motel room about to rape your daughter." The words made my stomach turn to say them, never mind remember seeing him stand over her, trying to pull her panties down her lifeless limbs.

Dre's dad's mouth dropped open. "So I dragged him into the bathroom and we had a conversation that ended in him pissing himself and me putting a bullet in his brain. Honestly? I'd do it all over again, especially after I found out that Conner and his buddy Eric decided that a nice gang bang against her will would be a super fun way to steal Dre's virginity."

Mr. Capulet paled.

"Last night it was Eric. We thought he was dead but he was the one responsible for what happened tonight. He got himself clean. Found Jesus, and took everything that was fucked up in his life out on Dre, but it was me he wanted to get to for killing Conner. Revenge and all that. Dre was just a tool to get to me," I said, feeling spent, emotionally and physically. I leaned back in my chair, propped my elbow on the armrest and dropped my forehead onto my fist.

"Where is Eric now?" he asked, like if he wasn't dead he'd bring him back to life and kill him all over again.

Our eyes locked. "Hell."

He coughed and covered his mouth with his closed fist. "Andrea knows all this? About Eric, about you?"

"Every damn thing. And the thing is that she's never asked me to change or be anyone else other than exactly who I am. Which is good because in some ways I'll always be the same, but in other ways I see things differently. Clearer. And I think it's all because of her. It's funny. I changed not because she wanted me to, but…"

"Because she didn't need you to," Mr. Capulet finished for me.

He didn't react. Didn't say a word. He glanced from floor to ceiling. From Dre to me, seemingly lost in his own thoughts.

The silence between us seemed to go on forever.

The beeping of the monitors and the occasional footsteps of passing hospital staff were the only sounds echoing throughout the tiny hospital room.

I must have drifted off because when I opened my eyes I was still in the hospital. Dre was still in the bed. The only thing that had changed was that Mr. Capulet was now standing above my chair, looking down at me with a pained expression on his face.

Without saying a word, he pulled me up into a forceful hug. One so hard it was almost like he was kicking my ass and embracing me at the same time. He finally let me go and sat back down.

"I totally get it if you fucking hate me. I failed her." I lowered my face into my hands and spoke through my fingers. "More than once. I should have just let her go. Let her stay and have a normal life. Find a normal guy," I said, but even as the words left my mouth they felt wrong. She was mine. Even if she'd left and found a normal guy, she would still be mine.

"You didn't fail me or her, son. Quite the opposite," Mr. Capulet said.

"How can you say that?" I glanced up. "This is all my fault. I'm the reason she's in this place. I'm the reason she's in a world of hurt. I'm the reason why she wound up in the hospital the first time. I'm even the reason why she can't get...why we can't..." I stopped and clenched my fists.

"Why she can't get pregnant?"

"Yeah," I said softly.

He shook his head. "No son, you're not the reason, although I still owe you a swift kick to the nuts for knocking up my daughter, I truly believe everything happens for a reason. If it wasn't for that incident. That moment in her life. If you would never have met her and she never lost the baby, she might never have gotten clean. Plus, she's told me what you've done for her. How you saved her on more than one occasion. And I don't hate you, son. I far from hate you. Andrea and I spoke a lot while she was back home. She's a strong girl and she's capable of making her own choices. She chose you for a reason. I'm not saying there is an excuse for what she's done in the past. I don't even think being an addict is really a proper term to describe her."

"What word would you use?" I asked, because I'd often thought the same thing.

Mr. Capulet smiled. "Human."

"Still. She's given me so much. I haven't given her shit."

"I wouldn't say that, son. You've given her more than you know."

"Oh yeah? Like what?"

"You said she knows all of it, right? Everything?" he asked.

"Yeah," I answered. "She does."

"Well then you've given her you. There isn't much more to give her than that."

"Sometimes I wonder what good am I?"

"To her? You're priceless."

I looked back over to my wife. Who was going to live and I finally felt like some of the weight bearing down on my soul was starting to lift.

"You've also given her something I never could," he added.

I spun around. "Yeah? What's that?"

His eyes gleamed with unshed tears. "Happiness, son. Happiness." He pinched his nose and wiped his eyes, changing the subject. "You know, you should write your story down someday. Write your memoirs. You've got some interesting stuff there."

I scoffed at the idea. "Yeah, and what would I call it? Alive Preppy, Dead Preppy?"

He set his hand on my shoulder. "I have a good title."

It would never happen. My life was too all over the place. It couldn't be contained inside of a book, but even I had to admit, the name he suggested had a certain ring to it.

The Life and Death of Samuel Clearwater.

★ ★ ★

DRE

A NURSE WOKE ME up at one point while Preppy was sleeping to draw some blood and she confirmed that despite my injuries, the baby growing inside of me was still there. Safe and sound.

I drifted off and when I woke again I was not met with just one, but two smiling faces.

One little. One big.

Both mine.

I have to tell you something, Bo signed to me.

"Bo, we can all talk later. You don't have to tell her now," Preppy started.

"No, it's okay," I said. "What do you want to tell me, Bo?"

He surprised me by crawling onto the bed and wrapping his arms around my neck in a tight hug, his head on my non-injured shoulder. I looked at Preppy and smiled, happy to be with my boys again. "A hug is definitely telling me something my beautiful boy," I said, kissing his temple.

Bo shook his head against me.

"No? That's not it?" I asked. I released my hold on him so he could sit up to sign to me, but he only snuggled into me further. "Bo, what is it you wanted to..." I started, but I didn't finish because the most beautiful little voice interrupted me when it began to whisper in my ear.

"I love you, Mommy."

My soul and heart leapt together and high-fived. I have something to tell you too," I said. I looked right at Preppy when I whispered to Bo. "Mommy's going to have a baby."

CHAPTER TWENTY-THREE

DRE

THREE MONTHS LATER

"**B**O'S COUNSELOR IS coming over in an hour," I told Preppy who was leaning against the counter with his shirt hanging open, ogling me like I was naked instead of covered in flour from head to toe. A side effect from baking Mirna's famous chocolate chip cookies combined with an unfortunate mixer malfunction. "Ray's going to drop him off after she picks him and Sammy up from school."

"Good," Preppy said, his eyes on the swell of my breasts. "He finished his work this morning so that works."

"Are you ever going to tell me what exactly you have him doing back there?" I asked, taking a damp rag to the counter.

"I told you. He's working on his punishment," Preppy answered, coming to stand behind me with his hands on my hips.

"Yes, I know. But what KIND of punishment. Like cleaning his room? Or like hard labor?" I asked, leaning back into his touch while I continued to clean. "I mean, how do you punish a kid for something like that?"

"I've got it handled, Doc," Preppy whispered against my ear, his hands resting on the burgeoning bump of my belly.

After Bo took an axe to Eric's head it didn't take us long to put two and two together since his biological mom was also found with an ax to her head. "I still can't believe that our boy, our little kind soul, killed two people."

"He's still a good kid. We just have to handle him right to make sure he knows right and wrong, but doesn't feel too much guilt about it. I told you. I've been there. I've got this," Preppy assured me.

I spun in his arms. "I trust you. You know I do. But can you please tell me what you have him doing in his room for an hour every day?"

Preppy grabbed my hand and led me down the hall. "You know how back in the day the teachers would make the kids copy a sentence a thousand times as their punishment? Like I WILL NOT PULL LITTLE GIRL'S HAIR?" Preppy pushed open the door to Bo's room. "Well, that's what he's been doing and what he will be doing for the rest of the school year. I haven't erased today's punishment just yet."

"Holy shit," I said, as I stared at the words written over and over again on the chalk-paint wall I'd made for him.

I will not kill anyone with an axe without permission.

"Without permission?" I asked.

Preppy leaned against the doorframe. "I mean, I didn't want to rule it out entirely. It kind of saved our asses that last time."

That was true, but it didn't change the fact that I couldn't tear my eyes from the words on the wall.

Preppy pulled me into his chest and kissed my hair. "Listen Doc, if anyone knows this, it's me. There's no black and white.

Right or wrong. What Bo did is in the grey-ish area. Together we're going to teach him how to be a good man, which means knowing how to be loyal to those who matter. When to sacrifice where it counts. And how to keep his promises. I want to show him what he did was wrong so he doesn't think he can go around offing anyone who pisses him off but I don't want to make him feel too guilty for something I really want to pat him on the back and buy him a pony for."

"We can do this," I said, letting Preppy's words sink in.

"Together. Okay?" he asked, rubbing his hands down my arms.

"Okay," I agreed. Preppy was right. Together we could teach Bo what was really important. That his past won't dictate his future. That the things you do don't define who you are.

That family runs thicker than blood.

Blood you'd spill for them, even if it's your own.

Bo came sprinting into the room and threw his arms around us, making our hug of two into a family affair.

I glanced from Preppy to Bo who were both resting a hand over my belly. We'd teach him that family was everything.

And we had it all.

★ ★ ★

PREPPY

DRE IS A fucking miracle worker. After she recovered from her injuries she followed through with the purchase of the house she wanted to renovate with the help of a realtor who didn't want to murder her or our family. She was five months pregnant and on her hands and knees in the house, tacking some of the broken baseboards back into place.

"You need to stop working so hard," I said picking her up off the floor. "Why isn't Kevin helping?"

"He is. He's been here all day," she said. Kevin was still living at our house and was giving Dre a hand when he wasn't working for me. "He just ran to the hardware store."

"Good. I don't like the idea of you here alone," I said.

"It's almost done," Dre beamed, looking around at the new paint on the walls, the freshly sanded floors, and the brand new windows with the stickers still on them.

"It looks fantastic." I dropped my gaze to her tits, which I couldn't get enough of normally, but now that they were swollen it was like they were calling to me all hours of the day and night.

Preppy come play with us

Preppy come fuck us

"The realtor has someone interested already and it's not even done, can you believe it?" she asked happily, her tits shaking as she bounced excitedly from foot to foot.

"I can believe it," I said, tipping her chin to me. "Because I believe in you."

"So are you going to tell me? Or what?" Dre asked, knowing I'd just came from a hearing at the county. I was officially the first licensed medical marijuana grower in the state. King, Bear, and I were going legit…ish.

"We got it," I told her, not able to hide my smile.

"Holy shit!" she leapt into my arms and wrapped her legs around me, sending a jolt of awareness down to my cock when her heat brushed up against me.

Her eyes darkened and she bit her lip. I backed her up

against the wall. "What do you say we start a new tradition?"

"What's that?" she asked as I ground my hard cock against her softness.

"I think this house needs to be christened." I gripped her ass tighter, making her very aware of my intentions.

Her moan was the only response I needed. Within seconds I'd stripped her of her shorts and had her lying against the stairs while I drove into her tight pussy over and over again until our screams echoed throughout the empty house.

I fell to the side of her and rested my head on her tits. I traced my fingers over her little belly.

"I still can't believe I'm actually pregnant," she said, watching me.

I scoffed. "I can't believe you underestimated the power I was packing."

"Hmmmmm. I think I'm still underestimating it." I glanced up at her. "Do you think you can show me this power you speak of again?"

My cock jumped to attention almost as fast as I did.

"Fuck yeah I can." I slide back into my wife, feeling love, happiness, and never more alive. I'd continue to make sure she'd feel every ounce of love I had for her. I made her promises that I'd keep or die trying.

~~Until~~ Not even death do us part.

EPILOGUE

PREPPY

ONE MONTH LATER

"SHIT," I SWORE. Jumping when pancakes shoved his cold nose against the back of my pant leg. I'd almost dropped the box I'd been carrying, my shoulder still weak from the gunshot wound, but overall it was healing nicely. I pointed at Pancakes. "Dude, it's frowned upon to come at someone from behind without proper warning, trust me, I know these things," I scolded.

King appeared in the doorway. "He's always doing that. It's kind of his thing," he said. The coyote darted out the door and disappeared. "Guess he doesn't like being told what to do either."

"Guess not," I agreed.

King followed me over to my car.

"So tell me this Boss-Man. Did Bear think he's such a big biker bad ass that he couldn't just go get a regular dog at the pound like a normal person?" I asked. "I mean he could have gotten a lab or a poodle, or even one of those ones that mixes the two, a labradoodle or some shit. No. The motherfucker had to go get himself a goddamned coyote."

King snickered. "This coming from the guy with a giant pig?"

"Oscar's the shit man. Seriously, though. I'm getting Bear a goldiepoo or some shit for Christmas."

"You settled down and now you're an expert on the perfect family dog?"

"Once you're married you'll understand," I said sarcastically.

"Oh that? We got tired of putting it off, so we just went and did the thing," King said like it was no big deal. I noticed a tattoo on his hand I'd never noticed before with Ray and the kid's names linked together around his ring finger.

"Oh yeah, that…Wait, what! You did what?" I asked. "And I wasn't invited?"

"Nobody was. It was the day we stuck you with the kids. I was getting tired of having her not be my wife and she told me she didn't want the shindig so we just did it. Now she's Mrs. Brantley King and I'm an old married man just like you."

"Wow, congrats, man," I said. "Do you think when Bear gets married he's gonna have the full out biker wedding with brawls and revving engines during the ceremony?"

"Probably," King agreed.

"I wonder if he'll wear a shirt…"

"So you finally came to get the rest of your shit?" King asked, pointing to the box in my arms.

I set it down in my trunk and slammed it shut, brushing the dust off my hands by clapping them together. "Yeah, figured it didn't do you any good to have it lying around here taking up space when I'm not living here anymore."

King and I both leaned up against my trunk. He lit a cigarette and passed me his lighter so I could do the same.

"I know I've been gone for a bit and I still come over pretty much all the time," I said, looking up at the house that had been my home for ten years, minus several months in Narnia. "And it feels weird to say this, but I'm gonna miss this place. I think leaving some of my shit here made it feel like I hadn't really moved out, not all the way. Now? Now it all feels really fucking real."

"What are you going to miss about it the most? The parties? Girls? All the bad fucking decisions we made?" King asked with a smile. He took a long drag of his cigarette, ashing it onto the gravel.

"Hey, I'll have you know that some of my favorite memories started with those bad decisions," I pointed out. "I feel the need to defend all of the ridiculous fun we had here."

"You remember the day we moved in?" King asked, looking up at the house.

"Like it was yesterday."

"It was a good day," King said.

I scratched my nose and waved the smoke from my eye. "It was the BEST fucking day ever, Boss-Man," I agreed. "The BEST."

King nodded and we both just stood there, staring at the house as if we were waiting for it to chime in with an opinion. The day we moved in really was a great day. Neither one of us owned much so when we moved from the roach infested apartment we'd been renting previously it only took one trip. And then it was just the two of us in an empty house with an old boom box. We took turns choosing songs to play while swigging from the bottle of whiskey and snorting lines off the kitchen counter.

"We were just a couple of stupid kids back then," I said. "It was so run down then." I pointed to the fresh paint and new siding. "I like what you've done with the place. How you and Ray have fixed it all up. It looks more adult and less 'hey lots of illegal shit going down inside.'"

King snickered. "It was a great house then and it's a great house now. It's just a different kind of great." He cocked his head to the side. "You know that you can build out the rest of the garage if you guys want to stay here with the fam. There could be room for everyone. I mean, shit, you can build all the way to the seawall if you want. It's your house too you know. Always has been." King lowered his voice. "You don't gotta live anywhere else."

I put a hand on King's shoulder. "I think that's the most consecutive sentences I've ever heard you speak at one time," I deadpanned.

King punched me in the arm and I rubbed it, pretending like he'd actually hurt me. Although in reality, it stung like a motherfucker, but I'd never let him know that.

"You know what I fucking mean, Prep," King said. "I don't want you to think you can't be here. You know, 'cause Ray wants you here."

"Oh, RAY wants me here. Is that it?" I teased. "No one else."

"Yup. Just her. I think you should get the fuck off my drive-way," King said, throwing me a side-glance, his shoulders shook as he silently laughed at his own joke.

I sighed. "It's not like I'm on the other side of the moon. I'm only a few blocks away. I tell you what, when you get sad and lonely and need your Preppy fix you can come cuddle with me if you get tired of cuddling that fine ass woman of yours," I said.

"I don't see that happening," King said with the kind of grin plastered on his face he didn't even own before Ray showed up.

"Yeah, I didn't think so," I agreed.

King sighed. "Well, if you insist on leaving then I have something for you. Two things actually." He shoved two paper sized yellow envelopes into my hands.

"What the fuck is this?" I asked, turning it over to inspect it. "Anthrax?"

"Yeah, Prep. Your moving out gifts are envelopes full of deadly poison," King said flatly. "Just fucking open them."

"Hey, you always gotta ask," I said, opening the top and peering inside. "What the fuck is all this?" I pulled out one of the baseball sized rolls of cash among about a dozen other thick stacks of hundreds.

"I told you," King said. "It's always been our house. We bought it together. Put the same money, sweat, and elbow grease into the place." He pointed to the cash. "You're moving on, so that's your half of what the place is worth."

"I think you're way over estimating the value," I argued. "There's way too much in here."

Although to me it would always be priceless.

King pushed his hands in his back pockets. "That's because it's also your split of everything, from when you were gone. Besides, you're about to be a dad again. You're gonna need it."

"Boss-Man," I started. "You don't have to." I held out the envelope for him to take it. "I never expected you to do this. I don't need you to give me any fucking money. I still got a shit ton of guilt money left anyway. And you're right, this place has always been ours. Whichever of us lives in it doesn't even matter to me. This...this never even crossed my fuckin' mind."

"I know it didn't," King said, refusing to take it back. "But it's yours anyway. I ain't taking it back."

"Thanks, Boss-Man," I said shoving the cash back in the envelope and tucking it under the crook of my arm.

"So what's this one?" I asked, shaking the second envelope and listening for any tell tale signs of its contents shaking around.

"Anthrax," King deadpanned.

"You're getting funny in your old age."

King glanced down at his phone. "I gotta go get the kids. Open that when you get home." He held out his hand, but instead of bro hugging him like he was expecting, I pulled him in for the real deal. We stood there for a moment, below the steps of the house we bought together the second we could scrape up the cash, with neither one of us in a rush to let the other go.

When we pulled back we didn't make eye contact, and it was totally because of the pollen in the air that was triggering my allergies making my eyes water. King must have had the exact same allergies, which was the reason why he was sniffling. "Thanks," I said again, not knowing what else I could say to him. He'd already given me so much. More than he could ever know.

He defended me when no one else would.

He protected me when I couldn't protect myself.

He became family when I didn't have one.

King shrugged and cleared his throat. "You would have done the same for me," he said, casually.

I smiled and finally met my friend's watery gaze. "No. No, I fucking wouldn't have." We both burst out in an uncontrollable fit of laughter.

It was totally our laughter that triggered the allergy induced tears to stream down our faces as we hugged it out again before I finally turned and got in the car without looking back. And it was totally the laughter again that was the reason why I had to pull over on the side of the road less than a block away to spend ten minutes wiping my stupid leaking face so I could see well enough to drive the rest of the way home.

Fucking allergies.

Fucking laughter.

When I finally pulled back onto the road I glanced up into the rearview mirror and watched the house on stilts, the one King and I dreamed about owning as kids, the first real home I'd ever had, grow smaller and smaller behind me. I sniffled and wiped my nose with the back of my hand.

I was still in my car, idling in the driveway at the house I now called home, when I opened the second envelope from King. I pulled out a picture frame. The actual frame wasn't anything special, but what was inside of it WAS. It was the drawing King and I had drawn together in my notebook on the day we met on the playground as two kids who didn't know shit about life except that it could be cold and cruel. I ran my fingertips over stick figure King and Preppy, then the Star Wars stilt home. I laughed at the blood spattered on the page from my broken nose and made a mental note that Tyler, the bully responsible for that bloody nose, was long overdue for a house egging. I read over our notes in misspelled block lettering. **HOBBIES** was in bold letters with **King: art shit** and **Preppy: bitches** written underneath. Next to **HOBBIES** was **GOALS**. Underneath we'd written: **Own the town. Be our own bosses.**

Kill anyone who gets in our way.

That day changed everything.

It changed ME.

King and I entered that playground as kids with no futures. We left with one we'd created.

Scribbled on the bottom of the frame, in bold black marker, in King's shitty handwriting, was a single sentence.

We did it all, and more.

"Yes, yes we motherfucking did," I said out loud, blinking back fresh tears and smiling like a crazed idiot.

Fucking best friends.

THE MOTHERFUCKING END

Author's Note

Dear Amazing Readers,

Writing the King Series has been one wild and crazy ride. Thank you for going on it with me. Thanks for embracing the characters and their stories. King, Bear, Preppy, Ray, Thia, and Dre thank you for your love.

When I released my first book, The Dark Light of Day, I never thought a single person would ever read a word I wrote. It was a dream of mine just to release a book and that was enough for me.

But then there was you.

Readers.

MY readers.

You demanded more of me. It took me a while but I gave you all I had and then some with King.

I've grown a lot throughout these last NINE books and you've been right there with me every step of the way. You've supported me. You've laughed with me. You've cried with me.

YOU have made my dreams come true.

I'm crying now as I type this to you. This may be the end of the main King series, but I have some spin-off's planned. I'll never say that I'm absolutely not going to ever revisit these characters again, because that's too final and I don't know what stories they may try to tell me in the future.

This is by NO MEANS the end of T.M. Frazier though. I PROMISE that if you continue to stick with me, I'll continue to stick with you and pour everything I've got into my stories.

Thank you for demanding more.

Humbly Yours,

T.M. Frazier

PS – Come join my Facebook readers group, FRAZIERLAND. It's the best group of readers EVER!

Other Books by T.M. Frazier

STANDALONE NOVELS
THE DARK LIGHT OF DAY – A King Series Prequel
(Jake & Abby's Story)
ALL THE RAGE – A King Series Spinoff
(Rage & Nolan's Story)

KING SERIES
KING, Book 1
TYRANT, Book 2
(King & Doe's Story)
LAWLESS, Book 3
SOULLESS, Book 4
(Bear & Thia's Story)

PREPPY,
THE LIFE & DEATH OF SAMUEL CLEARWATER
PART ONE, Book 5
PART TWO, Book 6
PART THREE, Book 7
(Preppy & Dre's Story)

COMING SOON-ISH
THE LIST – A New Standalone
UP IN SMOKE – Standalone – A King Series Spinoff

About the Author

T.M. Frazier is a *USA TODAY* BESTSELLING AUTHOR best known for her *KING SERIES*. She was born on Long Island, NY. When she was eight years old she moved with her mom, dad, and older sister to sunny Southwest Florida where she still lives today with her husband and daughter.

When she was in middle school she was in a club called AUTHORS CLUB with a group of other young girls interested in creative writing. Little did she know that years later life would come full circle.

After graduating high school, she attended Florida Gulf Coast University and had every intention of becoming a news reporter when she got sucked into real estate where she worked in sales for over ten years.

Throughout the years T.M. never gave up the dream of writing and with her husband's encouragement, and a lot of sleepless nights, she realized her dream and released her first novel, The Dark Light of Day, in 2013.

She's never looked back.

For more information on her books and appearances
please visit her website
www.tmfrazierbooks.com

FOLLOW T.M. FRAZIER ON SOCIAL MEDIA

FACEBOOK:

facebook.com/tmfrazierbooks

INSTAGRAM:

instagram.com/t.m.frazier

TWITTER:

twitter.com/tm_frazier

For business inquiries please contact Kimberly Brower of Brower
Literary & Management.
www.browerliterary.com